Mail Order Magpie

Book 58 in Brides of Beckham

Kirsten Osbourne

Chapter One

Seth Clinkinbeard squinted against the glare of the Texas sun, its heat already merciless in the early hours. He stood atop a gentle rise, hands perched on his hips, surveying the bustling activity below. Men moved like clockwork among the cattle, their shouts and the bawling of steers stitching together the soundscape of the ranch. Seth nodded in quiet approval.

He wiped a bead of sweat from his brow with the back of a hand that had known countless callouses. The Stetson he wore cast a shadow over sharp eyes that missed nothing—a stray calf, a fence needing mending, or a hand slacking off. His face bore the brunt of the elements, etching lines of determination around his mouth and eyes.

As he descended toward the heart of the ranch, the fabric of his shirt clung to him. With every step, dust rose to cling to his pants and mingle with the sweat on his skin. But none of that mattered to Seth. His focus lay solely on the land stretching out before him—land he'd turn into the most prosperous ranch this side of Fort Worth.

Seth strode along the edge of a newly fenced pasture, his keen eyes scanning the horizon where his cattle grazed under the Texas sun. A group of ranch hands worked nearby, driving posts into the parched earth. He approached them, the rhythmic thud of mallets against wood punctuating each step.

"Looks sturdy," Seth called out.

"Thanks, boss. Just following your diagram," replied Jack, a young hand.

"Let's double-check those knots on the top wire," Seth suggested, pointing toward the end of the line. "We don't want any surprises come round-up."

"Got it, Seth," another hand chimed in, already making his way over to tighten the loops.

"Good work today, boys. Keep an eye on that western patch though," Seth added, wiping his brow. "I think we'll need to rotate the herd come next week. The grass is wearing thin."

"Will do, boss!" Jack said.

As Seth continued his walk toward the barn, he spotted David leaning on the corral, watching a chestnut mare trot in circles. David was his closest neighbor, and their houses were close, though their ranches were vast. The horse kicked up dust that danced in the light breeze, and a smile tugged at Seth's lips. David had a way with animals that Seth could only admire.

"Fine day for training, isn't it?" Seth greeted, joining his friend by the fence.

"Gets better with every sunrise," David replied, pushing his hat back. "You've built a fortress here, but you forgot something important."

"What's that?" Seth quirked an eyebrow, his hands resting on the weathered wood.

"A wife, Seth. This land needs a woman's touch, and you need an heir." David's voice held a note of gentle prodding.

"An heir, huh?" Seth mused, his gaze drifting across the fields. "There's truth to that. But a wife requires finding the right one—someone who understands this life."

"Maybe she's closer than you think. Could be you just need to open your eyes to the possibilities," David said, a knowing look crossing his features.

"Perhaps," Seth conceded, the hint of a smirk playing at the corner of his mouth. "But for now, there's a ranch to run, and sunset waits for no man."

"True enough," David laughed, clapping Seth on the shoulder. "Just remember, even the hardest soil can nurture if tended right."

Seth nodded, his thoughts lingering on David's words as he watched the mare circle once more, her coat shining like burnished copper in the fading light.

Seth hurried into the cool shade of the barn. He pulled off his hat, wiping his brow with the back of a hand.

"Jake," Seth called out, spotting his foreman organizing tools by the workbench.

"Seth," Jake replied, straightening up with a nod. "What can I do for you?"

"Need your thoughts on something," Seth said. "It's about this idea of finding a wife."

"Ah," Jake chuckled, scratching at his chin. "David's been talking to you again, huh?"

"Yep," Seth affirmed, his lips pressed into a thin line. "He's got it in his head that I need someone to help run things. Says I need an heir too."

"Can't say he's wrong," Jake said, his eyes twinkling with a hint of mischief. "A wife could be good for you—and for the ranch."

"Maybe so," Seth admitted, his tone matter-of-fact. "But it's gotta be practical. I'm not one for all that lovey-dovey nonsense. She needs to know her way around a kitchen, and...well, she has to be sturdy. Capable of bearing children."

"Sounds like you're looking for more of a breeding mare than a bride," Jake joked, but there was no malice in his voice.

"Suppose it does sound that way," Seth said with a half-grin. "But this is serious business, Jake. A man's legacy and all."

"Fair enough." Jake nodded, leaning back against the workbench. "Well, there's the Mueller girl. Good with animals, strong stock. And the Widow Harris—she's no spring chicken, but she's got experience, knows how to handle a household."

Seth pondered the suggestions, his gaze distant. "I'll consider them. But it's got to be the right fit. Someone who won't balk at hard work or the Texas heat."

"Take your time, Seth. She's out there somewhere," Jake said, clapping a calloused hand onto Seth's shoulder. "And when the time comes, we'll make sure the ranch is ready for a lady's touch."

"Appreciate it, Jake," Seth replied, tipping his hat back on as he stepped out of the barn and into the late afternoon sun. The prospect of marriage still seemed foreign, but if it was necessary for the ranch, then Seth would find himself a wife—one who understood the value of hard work and the simple beauty of the land just as he did.

SETH THUMBED THROUGH the ledger on his desk, his brows furrowed as he calculated the costs of the recent cattle drive. The numbers added up nicely, but there was a figure missing from his life's equation—a wife. He leaned back in his chair and let out a sigh, glancing around the sparse room that served as both office and living quarters.

"Mail-order brides," he muttered to himself, the term echoing an idea that had been percolating in his mind since his last conversation with Jake. Efficient, straightforward, no need for drawn-out courtships or dances he had neither time nor inclination for. It was a business transaction, plain and simple. And he remembered that David had told him Susan had been a mail-order bride. And David's sister-in-law had something to do with mail-order brides, though for the life of him, he couldn't remember what.

He stood up, the wooden chair creaking under the shift of his weight, and pulled his hat down over his eyes. Striding out of the house, he made his way into town, the sun casting long shadows behind him as he went to send a telegraph. David had given him the name of his sister-in-law who was a matchmaker back east.

"Need wife. Strong, capable. Send details." Seth spoke to the clerk, who transcribed his words with a rapid click-clack of the keys.

"Looking for love, are ya?" the clerk, Anthony Fennel, asked with a smirk.

"Practicality," Seth corrected, his tone firm but not unkind.

"Suit yourself," the clerk mumbled, handing over a copy of the message.

SETH OPENED A LETTER he'd received in response, the script flowing and feminine. It was from Elizabeth Tandy, who had been recommended by his friend, David, as a matchmaker.

"Dear Mr. Clinkinbeard," he read aloud, his voice steady. "I understand your desire for a partner who appreciates the demands of ranch life. I believe I can assist you in this endeavor."

Seth's lips quirked upward slightly as he continued through the letter. Mrs. Tandy had a way with words that painted a hopeful picture without straying from the practicalities of the arrangement. He admired that.

"Mrs. Tandy seems to know her business," he said to the empty room. He'd never talked to a matchmaker before, but he liked her approach to the task at hand.

Penning a reply took longer than he expected; choosing words didn't come as naturally as roping steers. But eventually, he wrote:

"Mrs. Tandy, your assistance is welcomed. Looking for a woman of sound health, domestic skills, and able to withstand the Texas summer. Awaiting your recommendations."

Sealing the letter, Seth couldn't help but feel a flicker of curiosity about the woman Mrs. Tandy might send his way. It was a strange sensation, almost like the anticipation before a successful harvest. He shook it off and set the envelope aside to take into town to post the following day. He'd probably send Jack. For some reason, the fool did seem to like going to town.

"Let's see what you've got, Mrs. Tandy," he said quietly.

TWO WEEKS LATER, SETH received another letter from Mrs. Tandy.

"Dear Mr. Clinkinbeard," he read aloud, "I am pleased to inform you that a group of respectable young ladies will soon be arriving in Texas from the East Coast. They are eager to meet gentlemen such as yourself with the prospect of matrimonial union."

Seth's eyes flicked over the words, each sentence fueling a spark of curiosity he hadn't known was there. Would one of these girls hold the sturdy qualities he sought?

Chapter Two

Brenda Brown hummed a soft melody as she wove through the grand halls of the Harrington estate, her arms laden with toys and storybooks. The morning sun streaming through the windows cast a golden glow across her blonde hair. As she entered the nursery, a trio of eager faces looked up from their play, their laughter a bright echo in the spacious room.

"Brenda!" Junie, the youngest of her charges, exclaimed, her tiny hands clapping in delight.

"Good morning," Brenda greeted. She set the books down on the low table and began to distribute the toys, each child receiving exactly the one they hoped for. It was a small magic she performed daily, knowing their hearts.

"Will you read us a story?" Samuel asked, his brow furrowed with hopeful anticipation.

"Of course," Brenda said, her voice lilting with the promise of adventures bound within the pages. "But first, let's make sure everyone's hands are clean and faces are washed." She ushered them toward the washbasin, her practiced hands gently scrubbing away the traces of breakfast and play.

As the children settled around her, hanging onto every word of the tale she spun, Brenda couldn't help but feel a tug at her heartstrings. How she longed for children of her own, to kiss scraped knees and soothe nighttime fears. But daydreams were luxuries afforded to those with wealth, and Brenda knew her place.

The rest of the day unfolded with the comforting rhythm of routine. They played games in the garden, where Brenda chased after runaway balls and mended tattered doll dresses with equal fervor.

Lunch was a lively affair, with Brenda ensuring each giggling mouth was fed before seating herself with a modest plate.

"Miss Brenda, why don't you have lunch with the grown-ups?" Margaret, the eldest, asked between bites of her sandwich.

"Because I wouldn't dream of missing out on this delightful company," Brenda responded.

Afternoon lessons were next, and Brenda patiently guided quivering hands as they traced letters and numbers. Her praise was earnest and abundant, for she believed deeply in the power of encouragement. A scraped knee brought her to her feet, a tender touch and a bandage quickly dispelling tears.

"Better now?" she asked.

"Much better, thank you, Brenda," Samuel sniffled, already back to building his block tower.

Her day culminated with bedtime stories, whispered lullabies, and goodnight kisses pressed to foreheads. As darkness fell and the house quieted, Brenda lingered at the door, her gaze sweeping over the peaceful forms of the children. She turned off the light and closed the door softly behind her.

"Tomorrow is another day," she whispered to herself. And with that, she descended the stairs, the echoes of her footsteps a silent testament to the life she cherished and the dreams she dared to keep alive.

THE SUN WAS BARELY up when Brenda Brown stepped through the iron gates of the foundling home. It was her day off, so she'd spend it with those she loved. She relished these moments, the chance to reconnect with her family.

"Morning, Brenda!" piped a chorus of youthful voices as she entered the main hall, where breakfast was underway.

"Good morning," Brenda beamed, her presence sparking joy among the sea of young faces. Despite her blunt ways, the children adored her sincerity as much as she cherished their company.

"Brenda, will you braid my hair?" asked a small girl with unruly locks.

"Of course," Brenda assented, settling onto a bench with the child between her knees. Her fingers worked deftly, weaving the strands into a neat plait while the little ones gathered around. They knew her visits were special.

"Enough dawdling, children," came a voice both firm and kind. Mrs. Agatha Jackson stood at the threshold of the dining area.

"Good to see you, Brenda," she greeted, eyeing Brenda over the rim of her glasses. "I trust the little ones are treating you well?"

"Of course, Mrs. Jackson," Brenda replied, standing to face the matron with a respectful nod. The woman before her had raised her and even named her when she came to the foundling home, offering solace and stability in the chaotic world of an orphanage. Mrs. Jackson managed it all, from skinned knees to temper tantrums.

"Sometimes I wonder how much longer I can manage this place. I'm an old woman, Brenda!"

"Ah, but what would we do without you, Mrs. Jackson? I need you as much now as I did when I arrived here." Brenda mused aloud. A world without Mrs. Jackson's guiding hand was one none of them wished to contemplate.

"Run amok, no doubt," Mrs. Jackson said with a chuckle. "Now, go on and enjoy your day, Brenda. Heaven knows you've earned it."

With a final wave to the children and a promise to return soon, Brenda stepped out into the bright new day, carrying with her the warmth of her orphanage family and the unwavering support of the woman who held it all together.

Brenda went into the kitchen to go out through the door there. She wanted to spend some time outside on her day off.

"Off to see the world, are you?" Amy asked as she caught sight of Brenda. Her hands were dusted with flour, evidence of her latest kitchen endeavor.

"Only if 'the world' is our little corner of it," Brenda replied with a grin. Amy looked every bit the elder sister she was. Amy had been the first orphan who had been left as an infant with no name when Mrs. Jackson had become matron of the foundling home. Mrs. Jackson had named all the girls in alphabetical order, starting with Amy. The boys had been named from Z through A starting with Zachary.

"Actually, I've got news," Amy said, suddenly serious. "Mrs. Jackson's been cooking up a plan. We're going to Texas."

"Texas?" Brenda asked, her eyebrows arching in surprise. "What's in Texas?"

"A matrimonial opportunity," Amy began. "There's a church outside Fort Worth. They're hosting a big matchmaking party. Men with land and no wives. Women wanting husbands. They're looking for girls willing to take the chance."

"Matchmaking?" Brenda pondered the strange and thrilling concept. "So, you mean to say we could find husbands there? Real ones?"

"Absolutely," Amy confirmed. "And not just any husbands. Ranchers, farmers—men with roots. Men who need strong women beside them. There's a matchmaker in Beckham who came and talked to Mrs. Jackson about potentially sending girls from here as mail-order brides. Mrs. Jackson won't let us go to marry someone sight unseen, but she's willing to agree to the party, and she's gathering interested girls who are over eighteen. Poor Jane wants to go but she won't be eighteen until August. Mrs. Jackson said she can join later."

Brenda's heart quickened at the thought. She had always craved love, the kind that would root her to a place and give her a family of her own. "Oh, Amy," she said, her eyes dancing with possibility. "I want to be a part of this. More than anything."

"Thought you might," Amy said, smiling knowingly. "You've got that fire in you, Brenda. A passion for life. Those Texans won't know what hit them when you step off that train!"

"Then it's settled!" Brenda declared, her voice thrumming with determination. "We'll go to Texas, and we'll find those husbands!"

"Let's hope they know what they're in for," Amy laughed. "The Brown sisters are coming, and we aren't the wilting sort."

"Never have been, never will be," Brenda agreed, her laughter mingling with Amy's as they shared a moment of spirited camaraderie. Together, they would embark on an adventure beyond the safe confines of Massachusetts, and they'd face the unknown.

BRENDA TIED THE LAST ribbon on her well-worn carpetbag with a firm tug, her fingers steady despite the flutter in her chest. The noise of the bustling orphanage echoed around her.

When she'd tried to give two weeks notice to the Levitts, they had given her an ultimatum. Stay on or leave immediately. It was easier to just leave, though she'd managed to say goodbye to the children. Mrs. Levitt had been to the foundling home twice, hoping she'd go back to them, but Brenda yearned for a new beginning, and she was going to get it.

"Are you ready, Brenda?" Mrs. Jackson asked as she stood by the door.

"Ready as I'll ever be, ma'am," Brenda replied, her eyes shining with resolve.

"Texas won't know what hit it," Elizabeth Tandy chimed in from behind, her tone light and teasing.

A smile tugged at Brenda's lips. She'd gotten to know Mrs. Tandy a bit in the two weeks since she'd left her job. She rather liked the woman, and she was pleased Mrs. Tandy was doing all she could for them. "Let's hope they're ready for a whirlwind," Brenda said.

The other girls buzzed with nervous energy, chattering about the life that awaited them. But Brenda's mind was focused on the prize. A husband and someday children. Who could ask for more in life?

"Train leaves at dawn. We all need to sleep," Mrs. Jackson instructed. "Tomorrow begins a new chapter for all of you."

"Thank you, Mrs. Jackson," Brenda said, her gratitude genuine. "You've given us a chance at something...real."

"Child, helping you find your way is my heart's work," the matron answered.

"Will it be hot there?" Imogene asked seeming both excited and worried.

"Hotter than any of us can imagine," Brenda assured her with a grin. "But we're made of strong stuff."

"Indeed, we are," Elizabeth agreed, patting the girl's hand.

Brenda lay on the floor, staring up at the wooden ceiling, her mind full of possibilities. She would miss the children she'd nannied, their laughter and innocent mischief. But ahead was the great unknown, a chance to carve out her world, to finally have a family of her own.

"Tomorrow, Texas," she whispered. "I'm coming for you."

GETTING TO THE TRAIN station the following morning was an adventure in and of itself. The girls scrambled around to wash their faces and get their bags downstairs.

There were so many of them, and most ended up riding in the back of the wagon with no seats. Brenda was thankful she was in front with Amy, her closest friend and confidante.

An entire herd of cows crossed the road in front of them just before they reached Beckham, Massachusetts, and Brenda was afraid for a moment they would be too late and miss their train, but the cows finally crossed and they were on their way again.

When a freight wagon was parked in front of the station, Brenda thought she might scream, but she swallowed down her anger, jumped down from the wagon with her carpetbag, and told the other girls it was time to get there. She rushed toward the platform.

All nine of the girls and Mrs. Jackson jumped down, leaving a man from their church to drive the wagon back to the foundling home.

They immediately spotted Mrs. Tandy. "Are we all ready for the adventure of our lives?" she asked.

Brenda grinned. She knew a lot of the others were scared, but she was only excited. She was starting a new life. A life that would be filled with love, laughter, and many children, who would grow up to marry Amy's children of course. What else would children do?

Chapter Three

Brenda's heart raced as she stepped onto the train, her hand gripping the worn leather handle of her carpet bag tightly. The steam hissed and the metal beast seemed to beckon her forward with a promise of new beginnings. Excitement bubbled up inside her, and she watched the other girls who were all so nervous about the prospect of their marriages.

"Here we go," she whispered to herself.

"Right behind you, Brenda," Amy said.

The wooden benches in the train car were hard and unyielding, but Brenda barely noticed as she settled next to Amy. Across from them sat Mrs. Jackson and Elizabeth Tandy, both beacons of maternal warmth and professional poise. Mrs. Jackson's gray curls peeked out from her bonnet, a soft smile on her lips, while Elizabeth looked every inch the matchmaker in her crisp blouse and skirt, her green eyes dancing with secrets of the heart.

"Mrs. Tandy?" Brenda began, eager to ask some questions. "I think this whole matchmaking business is quite an adventure."

"Yes, it has its moments. Now, sit back. We've got a long ride ahead."

"Mrs. Jackson," Amy asked, "do you think it'll be very hot in Fort Worth? All I've ever heard about Texas is how very hot it is."

"Hotter than you can imagine," Mrs. Jackson said. "I've never been, but it's all I've heard about Texas as well."

"Good thing we're not made of sugar," Brenda said, her eyes twinkling. "We won't melt too easily."

"Speak for yourself," Amy said. "I'm as sweet as you are sour."

Brenda laughed, playfully elbowing Amy. "That wasn't sweet!"

"I never said I was perfect," Amy said.

"I can see you two are going to do just fine. But to answer your previous question, Fort Worth's heat is overwhelming, but the community you'll be part of there is absolutely wonderful," Elizabeth said. "You'll see what I mean when we arrive. I went out there because I was in danger, and I married my husband along the way. My sister was our hostess, and she invited us to go to church with them. It was just lovely."

The clack of the train against the tracks set a rhythm to their journey, each click a step closer to what might be the biggest change in Brenda's life. She watched the world blur by through the open window, the wind tangling her blond hair as she leaned into the possibility of love and companionship.

"Adventure awaits, doesn't it?" Brenda mused aloud, more to herself than anyone else.

"Indeed, it does," Elizabeth agreed.

As the train chugged toward Fort Worth, Brenda felt the threads of her old life begin to loosen, making way for the tapestry of tales yet to be woven under the vast Texas sky.

BRENDA LEANED HER ELBOW on the window ledge, the passing scenery a blur of greens and browns. "So, Mrs. Tandy," she began with a tilt of her head, "how does one become a matchmaker?"

Elizabeth flashed a warm smile that crinkled the corners of her eyes. "Oh, my dear, it's all about understanding hearts more than minds. People come to me with their dreams of finding someone, and I do my best to make those dreams a reality."

"Must be quite the task," Brenda replied, genuinely intrigued.

"It is," Elizabeth answered, tucking a strand of hair behind her ear. "But nothing compares to seeing two people find happiness together. I once matched one of my younger sisters, who preferred to run around town barefoot and covered in mud, to a banker in Boston. You've never seen a more mismatched couple in your life!"

Brenda chuckled. "And how did that go?"

"Surprisingly well," Elizabeth beamed. "They both learned to compromise and fell in love. They're expecting their first child."

"Really?" Brenda raised an eyebrow. "That's something."

"Something wonderful," Elizabeth corrected. "They've been happily married for a while now."

"Wow." Brenda mused. "That's not just luck then. You've got a gift."

"Perhaps," Elizabeth conceded with a modest shrug. "But it's more about listening and observing. I talk to the women who want to go west, and I do all I can to match them with men who will suit their circumstances. I read every letter, and I read between the lines to figure out what the man really needs in his life. I learned from a matchmaker who sent my sister Susan to marry a rancher near Fort Worth."

"Sounds like you give folks a real chance at happiness," Brenda said, her voice softening.

"That's the hope," Elizabeth replied. "Everyone deserves a bit of romance in their lives, don't you think?"

"Can't argue with that," Brenda smiled, feeling a flutter of excitement at the prospect of what awaited her in Fort Worth.

BRENDA LEANED IN, RESTING her chin on the palm of her hand as Elizabeth's stories wove through the soft clatter of the train. Her heart danced to the rhythm of possibility. "So," Brenda ventured, "how do you do it? The matchmaking?"

Elizabeth's eyes twinkled, and she clasped her hands together. "Oh, my dear, it starts with understanding the heart's desires," she began, shifting in her seat to face Brenda fully. "It's about more than just throwing two people together and hoping for the best."

"Compatibility, then?" Brenda guessed, her brows knitting together thoughtfully.

"Exactly!" Elizabeth affirmed. "You see, when two people share common ground—values, dreams, even their favorite pastimes—it creates a place where love can grow. Take two people and there is almost always something they have in common. You emphasize whatever that commonality is, and you have hope for them."

"I guess that makes sense," Brenda mused aloud, her mind painting pictures of shared smiles and intertwined hands.

"I look at their character, ask about how they treat others, and try to learn what makes them happy. It's those little details that tell me if two people might look at each other one day and realize they've found home."

"Home..." Brenda echoed, the word weaving hope around her heart. She pictured herself laughing beside someone who understood her jokes, someone who saw the world through a lens similar to her own.

"Trust me," Elizabeth said, reaching out to give Brenda's hand a reassuring squeeze. "There's a magic in finding someone who shares your vision of the future, who values the same cornerstones of life."

Brenda smiled, her nervousness fading like stars at dawn. "Magic," she whispered, letting Elizabeth's confidence wash over her. As the train whistled its approach to Dallas, Brenda's thoughts fluttered to the dance awaiting them, to the chance of finding her match in a crowd of hopeful hearts.

"Let's find you that magic," Elizabeth said. "You deserve happiness."

"So, Mrs. Tandy," she started, tapping her fingers on her knee, "how exactly do you pick who suits who?"

Elizabeth's lips curved into a knowing smile as she leaned back against the plush train seat. "I received a letter from a man in the west, who signed the letter, the hungriest man in...Oh, I don't remember which state."

"So you sent him a hungry woman?" Brenda asked, eager for specifics.

Elizabeth laughed, shaking her head. "No, I sent him a cook, of course. That man fell in love with his wife one bite at a time."

"Really?" Brenda couldn't help but grin at the thought of such a meeting. "And they're happy together?"

"Very," Elizabeth confirmed. "Their mutual love for food, her for cooking it and him for eating it, made them both happy."

"Food," Brenda said, the idea planting itself in her imagination.

Brenda leaned back into the seat of the train, her heart aflutter like the wings of a caged bird eager for release. The rhythmic chug of the locomotive was a soothing backdrop to the dreams blossoming in her mind. "What if I really do meet him?" she mused aloud, her voice tinged with a hope she'd seldom allowed herself to feel.

"Your Prince Charming?" Elizabeth said, her tone playful yet sincere. She adjusted the brim of her hat, a small smile playing on her lips as she regarded Brenda. "I've seen it happen before, dear. Love has a way of showing up when we least expect it."

Brenda's green eyes sparkled with the reflection of the passing scenery. "But you truly think he's out there? A man who can handle my...well, my Brenda-ness?"

"Without a shadow of a doubt." Elizabeth's confidence was contagious, and Brenda felt it seep into her. "You're a remarkable young woman. Anyone would be lucky to have you by their side."

"Even with my stubborn streak?" Brenda asked, half jesting, half seeking reassurance.

"Especially with it," Elizabeth affirmed. "It shows you have a spine of steel. And trust me, that's something to be admired."

Nodding, Brenda let out a breath she hadn't realized she'd been holding. For the first time in what felt like forever, the future seemed not just a distant possibility, but a vivid promise waiting to unfold.

"Thank you," Brenda said. "For believing in a happy ending for me."

Elizabeth reached across the aisle, her hand covering Brenda's with a gentle warmth. "It's more than belief, my dear. It's a certainty. We'll find the one who complements your spirit, and together, you'll write your own love story."

The thought alone filled Brenda's chest with a lightness that bordered on elation. As the train drew nearer to its destination, Fort Worth no longer symbolized just a city but the gateway to a life she had only dared to wish for in whispers.

The train let out a final, lingering hiss as it came to a rest at the Fort Worth station. Brenda peered through the window, her eyes taking in the bustling platform alive with the energy of new arrivals and heartfelt farewells.

"Here we are," Elizabeth chirped, standing up and swaying for a moment as she got used to having her legs under her. This train ride had been measured in days and not hours, so it was strange to stand without the floor moving under her. "Fort Worth, the city of cowboys and culture. And , perhaps, romance."

Brenda couldn't help the smile that tugged at her lips. The infectious optimism of Elizabeth's voice made the butterflies in her stomach do a hopeful dance. They disembarked, the hot Texas air making Brenda wonder how hot it would be in July and August when it was this hot in early June.

"Remember to breathe," Elizabeth whispered as they stepped onto the platform. "Every great adventure begins with a single step – or in your case, a twirl at a dance."

"Let's hope my feet remember the steps," Brenda replied. She'd always enjoyed when they'd danced at the foundling home. It hadn't happened often, but it had been fun to spin in circles with boys she considered her brothers.

Elizabeth's sisters Susan and Alice were waiting at the train station, each of them with a wagon that extra boards had been laid on to create extra seats.

The drive to Susan's house took them out of the city into wide open spaces filled with ranches and farms. They drove past a church, and Susan pointed it out as the setting for the dance tomorrow evening.

When the wagon stopped in front of the ranch house, Brenda scrambled to the ground, excited. Hopefully, she would marry at the party, and they would go straight to her new home, and she would only spend a single night in the beautiful house in front of her.

Susan jumped down and spread her arms wide and Elizabeth flew into them. "Elizabeth," she said, looking at Mrs. Jackson and embracing her as well. "You must be Mrs. Jackson. We're going to get all your girls married off to good men. I promise."

"Thank you, Mrs. Dailey," Mrs. Jackson said, stepping inside, where the sounds of children's laughter echoed from the other room.

"Please, call me Susan. We only have one bathroom, so everyone will need to take turns using it. My housekeeper, Mrs. Hackenschleimer and I will be filling the tub in the kitchen as well." Susan led them upstairs to a room filled with more lace and frills than Brenda had ever seen.

TWO AT A TIME, THE nine young women from Massachusetts bathed in the grand house outside of Fort Worth, and they were each dressed in gowns Susan had borrowed from friends and neighbors for the occasion.

Brenda emerged from an upstairs bedroom, her cream-colored shirt adorned with delicate lace and a bright blue skirt that flowed around her. She couldn't deny the slight flutter in her stomach as she tucked a loose strand of hair behind her ear and prayed silently for the night to bring her the right man.

Her mind couldn't decide between confidence and nervousness, so she chose to be confident. She would find the right man, and she would be happy. Tonight, she would begin her forever.

Chapter Four

The sun was barely up when Seth Clinkinbeard's day erupted into a series of calamities. A fence line down in the south pasture, a mare near foaling in the north barn, and an ornery bull causing chaos among the heifers. He was a man more at home under the vast Texas sky than any roof, but today, it seemed even the land he loved was conspiring against him.

Frustrated, he grunted as he struggled with the uncooperative timber needed to repair the fence. His brow was covered in dust, and his shirt stuck to his back from the relentless summer heat. Seth was no stranger to hard work. However, dealing with these issues on such a scorching day was irritating him greatly.

"Can't believe I'm fussing over a doggone dance," he grumbled to no one in particular, hammering away his frustration with each determined strike.

He cast a critical eye over the last of his handiwork. It would hold. For now. Glancing at the pocket watch that rarely left his side, a curse slipped past his lips. The matchmaking party – a social affair he viewed as little more than a necessary nuisance – was set to begin in half an hour, and here he was, still wearing his work clothes and stinking to high heaven.

"Should be tending to the land, not prancing around some blasted dance floor," Seth scoffed, yet a sense of duty propelled him toward his homestead. The Clinkinbeard name carried weight in these parts, and skipping out on Elizabeth Tandy's well-intentioned shindig wasn't the right thing to do.

He took long strides, urgency etched into the lines of his face. The house stood silent. He dashed inside, mentally thanking his father for all the windows he'd installed, making the house a bit cooler than the outside.

"All right, Seth, make it quick," he murmured. Shedding his work clothes with haste, he splashed water from the basin onto his face, scrubbing away the evidence of the day's trials. He did his best to wash away any scents on him, but he didn't have time for a bath. He dressed swiftly, choosing a clean shirt and a pair of trousers that didn't smell.

"Whoever thought a man should have to don a tie in this heat ought to be hog-tied themselves," Seth complained, struggling with the unfamiliar fabric around his neck. With a final tug, the knot sat acceptably at his collar, and he surveyed himself in the small mirror hanging lopsided on the wall.

"Good enough," he decided with a resigned shrug. His appearance was rugged, and tonight it would have to suffice.

"Time to face the music," Seth said, tipping his hat onto his head as he stepped outside once more, the promise of the evening stretching out before him like the open range – vast, unpredictable, and mildly intimidating.

Seth rode his favorite gelding to the country church where the dance was to take place. He knew he was cutting it close, but his day had gotten away from him more than once. A dance wasn't worth all this fuss, he thought, but there had been no wriggling out of it. Not with David's matchmaking plans set on finding him a bride.

"Come on, girl," he urged his mount, patting her neck. "Just a bit further."

He swung down from the saddle outside the church hall, hitching his ride with practiced ease. Seth straightened his tie with a quick, rough pull and ran a hand through his hair in an attempt at taming the unruly locks. His heart hammered, not from the ride but the prospect of what awaited him inside. He was surprised at how very nervous he was.

Pushing open the doors, Seth stepped into the church. The room hummed with the low murmur of early arrivals, men gathered in loose clusters, speaking in tones that matched the casual air of the evening. His eyes scanned for familiar faces, and there, leaning against the back wall, stood David.

"Thought the night would be half over by now," Seth joked as he approached, the tension seeping from his shoulders.

David chuckled, his weathered face breaking into a knowing smile. "Figured I'd tell you the wrong time. Knew you'd be late otherwise."

"Tricky," Seth said, but he couldn't help the grin spreading across his face. "So, I'm on time?"

"Better than that, you're early. Ladies haven't even arrived." David's eyes twinkled with mirth. "We've got a meal first, then dancing. No need to rush through supper like it's a cattle drive."

"Guess I owe you one, David." Relief washed over Seth, bringing with it an unexpected lightness.

"I'll introduce you to the prettiest girl here," David replied, his tone teasing. "Then you'll owe me two. I like it when you owe me."

Seth groaned, shaking his head in amusement. They both knew he wouldn't find any joy in the bustling swirl of skirts and polite conversation. But tonight, maybe just for tonight, he could pretend there was nowhere else he'd rather be.

THE HOT SUMMER NIGHT made Brenda seriously second guess herself as she made her way up the steps of the small church. She paused for a moment, smoothing down her dress with slightly trembling hands. She felt her heart beating faster, and wished the sweat wasn't glistening off her face.

"Here goes nothing," she said to herself before pushing open the heavy wooden door. Her sisters were all behind her, happy to let her lead the way, but Brenda didn't mind. She was strong, and she was going to help her sisters where she could.

Inside, lanterns cast a golden glow across the faces of eager bachelors and hopeful maidens. The room buzzed with energy, each person present for the same reason. The promise of finding a partner for their lives. There were a few local women there to help make introductions and to provide food, but that's all they were doing. This dance was about her and her sisters finding mates.

Brenda's gaze swept through the crowd until it caught on a man who stood out from the rest. There was a man with broad shoulders straining against the fabric of his shirt. He looked to her as if he was uncomfortable in his suit and tie, but who could blame him? It was scorching hot. His hair was dark, tousled by the wind, and his eyes were dark. At least they appeared to be from across the room.

He wasn't the sort to fuss over appearances, evident by the scuff on his boots and the hint of stubble shading his strong jaw. Yet there was an unmistakable air of anticipation about him, a readiness that seemed to draw the room's attention.

Those hawk-like eyes found Brenda just as she stepped fully into the light of the hall, and for a moment, time seemed to slow. He watched her, not with the fleeting interest of a man at a party but with a focus that hinted at something deeper, something unspoken.

"Evening, Miss Brown," he called, his deep voice carrying over the chatter. Thankfully, David had been kind enough to tell him all the ladies were Miss Brown. That made things easier.

"Hello," Brenda replied. "You do not look like you want to be here."

"I don't," Seth said, a hint of a smile tugging at the corner of his mouth. "But I want a wife, and Mrs. Tandy wrote me a letter telling me to come here and meet single ladies. Where else would I go?"

"I'm sure I don't know!" Brenda said. "Who are you, anyway?"

He chuckled. "I guess me knowing that you and your sisters are all Miss Browns doesn't make it so you know my name. It's Seth. Seth Clinkinbeard."

"That last name is a mouthful. How long after a marriage would you give a lady to learn to spell it?"

"Oh, at least a week." Seth hadn't expected to be charmed by one of the ladies looking for a husband. Of course, he'd had no idea what to expect, but he liked this one. "And your first name, if you don't mind?"

"Brenda. My name is Brenda." She offered him her hand, and he surprised her by kissing it. The man looked like he should be out with his animals, not in a church turned event hall. But he had manners, and she liked that. She liked it a lot.

Brenda's eyes widened a touch as Seth's gaze settled on her, an intensity in his eyes that she hadn't anticipated. She felt a flutter in her chest. Tilting her head slightly, she took in his tall frame and rugged features, wondering what thoughts were running through his mind.

"See something you like?" Brenda asked, her tone light, as she approached Seth amidst the hum of the partygoers.

"I guess I do," Seth replied, the corners of his eyes crinkling with amusement.

"Well, then should we talk and get to know one another? I think we could be seated together for supper if we asked Mrs. Dailey nicely."

"No need to bother Mrs. Dailey," Seth said. "Her husband is a good friend of mine. He'll make it happen."

"That sounds nice then."

Seth leaned back against the wall, creating a small pocket of calm in the festive chaos.

"Truth be told, Miss Brown, I've got more cattle than sense when it comes to fancy gatherings like this," he admitted, his voice carrying a note of confession.

"Sounds like we're in the same boat, then," Brenda said, folding her arms. "I'd rather face a room full of rowdy children than try to make heads or tails of finding a husband."

"Then why come tonight?" Seth asked, genuinely curious about what drove a woman like Brenda to attend a dance aimed at tying bonds.

"I want a family of my own. Back east, I was a nanny for delightful children with awful parents." Brenda shrugged, her honesty laying bare her uncertainty.

"Fair enough," Seth nodded. "I'm here more out of obligation than want. The ranch needs a steady hand, and they say a wife's good for that."

"Seems a bit cold, don't you think? Reducing marriage to an employment application?"

"Maybe," he conceded, "but it's the truth. Not much for sweet talk or promises I can't keep."

"Can't fault a man for being honest," Brenda said, her green eyes reflecting a mix of respect and challenge. "But if it's just help you're after, why not hire more hands?"

"Hands are easy to find. Trust is rare," Seth said, his eyes meeting hers squarely. "A wife's someone to stand by you, through droughts and storms alike. And ranch hands can't bear my children."

"Suppose that's true," Brenda mused, the noise of the party fading into the background as they continued their earnest exchange. "But what about love? Does that factor into your equation at all?"

Seth hesitated, his brow furrowing. "Love's a luxury. Respect, loyalty, those are the things that keep a home standing."

"Maybe so," Brenda acknowledged, her heart wrestling with the idea of a practical union devoid of passion. "But even the hardiest of homes need a little warmth, wouldn't you say?"

"Perhaps you're right," Seth replied, and there was a softness in his voice that suggested he might just be open to the idea. "And I plan on keeping us both warm at night."

Brenda felt a shiver run through her. She'd kissed a few boys, and she'd liked it a great deal more than she should. She was a good girl, and she hadn't let herself do more than kiss, but she desperately wanted to know what came next. And he was outright promising her what would come next.

After dinner, a young man asked Brenda to dance, and she agreed, realizing there were two men for every woman at this dance. But as she danced with him, she thought of Seth.

At the end of the dance, she turned to look across the room to where Seth stood, a solitary figure against the backdrop of laughter and music. She couldn't help but imagine a life filled with the romance she'd read about in dog-eared novels, stolen moments beneath the Texas stars, and slow dances that lasted until dawn.

"You've got that look again," Elizabeth Tandy said, sidling up beside her with a knowing smile.

Brenda turned to the matchmaker, her face flushing with embarrassment. "What look?"

"The one of a woman dreaming of love, sweet love," Elizabeth teased gently. "But, honey, I see you've caught Seth's eye, and he's as practical as they come."

"Practical is fine for running a ranch, Elizabeth," Brenda sighed, "but what about the heart? Doesn't love have to enter into it somewhere?"

"Love can grow from the smallest seed, Brenda," Elizabeth replied, her green eyes sparkling with conviction. "Give it time, give it care, and who knows? You might just find yourself surprised."

"Surprised?" Brenda echoed, a half-smile tugging at her lips.

"Absolutely," the matchmaker affirmed. "Why, some of the strongest marriages I know started out as nothing more than agreements. Companionship is a fine place to start, and before you know it, affection blooms."

Brenda pondered this, her heart daring to hope. "So, you think Seth and I could…?"

"Could find joy in each other's company? Could build a life together that's about more than chores and cattle?" Elizabeth finished for her. "Yes, I do. But it takes two willing hearts, dear. Two hearts open to possibility."

"Maybe so," Brenda murmured, feeling the weight of Elizabeth's words. She glanced back at Seth, noticing how the light caught the edges of his rough-hewn features, and for a brief moment, she allowed herself to picture a life where practicality and passion intertwined.

Before she knew it, Seth was in front of her. "Miss Brown?" Seth's voice cut through the din, steady and sure.

She turned to face him, her green eyes meeting his. "Please, call me Brenda," she said.

"All right, Brenda."

They stood there, momentarily silent, the noise around them fading into a distant hum. Could something tender grow between them, or was she just setting herself up for disappointment?

"Mr. Clinkinbeard," she finally said, her voice a mix of steel and silk. "I think we're both here for the same reason."

Seth nodded, his brow furrowed ever so slightly. "To find someone who'll share the burdens and the joys of life."

"Joys?" she asked, her sharp wit getting the better of her nerves. "You talk as though you've got a list, and joy's just another item to be checked off."

He smiled then, and it was an unexpected sight. "Maybe I do, and maybe…just maybe, you're on it."

Brenda felt her heart stumble. Was this practical, money-minded rancher implying there might be room for more than mere convenience? She bit her lip, her inner turmoil raging like a prairie storm. All her life, she'd been the sturdy rock for her sisters, never allowing herself the luxury of romantic dreams. At least not where they could tell it was happening. But standing here, with Seth's earnest gaze locked on hers, the rock wavered.

"Are we really doing this?" she asked, searching his eyes for a clue that he shared even a sliver of her hope for something beyond a transaction.

"Seems to me," Seth began, shifting closer, "that we have a chance to make something work. Something real."

"Real," Brenda repeated. It wasn't love – not yet – but it was a start.

"Miss Brown, Brenda," Seth corrected himself with a half-grin, "I don't have all the answers. But I'm willing to try if you are."

She glanced around at the festive scene, the couples already dreaming of their futures together, and then back at the man before her.

"All right, Seth Clinkinbeard," Brenda said. "Let's give it our best shot."

"Repeat after me," Pastor Amos Kauffman's voice was clear, "I, Seth Clinkinbeard, take thee, Brenda Brown..."

Seth cleared his throat, his deep voice steady but tinged with an unfamiliar tremble, "I, Seth Clinkinbeard, take thee, Brenda Brown..."

"To be my wedded wife," the pastor continued, her eyes flicking between them, encouraging.

"To be my wedded wife," he echoed, glancing at Brenda, whose hands were surprisingly still in his.

"From this day forward," Pastor Kauffman said.

"From this day forward," Seth confirmed. His gaze didn't waver from Brenda's, and for a heartbeat, the rest of the world fell away.

"Repeat after me," Pastor Kauffman turned to Brenda, "I, Brenda Brown, take thee, Seth Clinkinbeard..."

Brenda's voice was less polished, but no less determined, "I, Brenda Brown, take thee, Seth Clinkinbeard..."

"To be my wedded husband," said the pastor.

"To be my wedded husband," Brenda said, and her voice held a note of wonder, as if she herself was surprised by the weight of it.

"From this day forward," Pastor Kauffman finished.

"From this day forward," Brenda repeated, her green eyes locked onto Seth's, finding something like resolve reflected back at her.

"By the power vested in me," Pastor Kauffman said in a loud voice that carried throughout the church, "I now pronounce you man and wife."

As Seth and Brenda turned to face the small gathering, a collective breath seemed to be released. Applause filled the room, yet all Brenda could hear was the rapid beat of her own heart. This was real. She was married. To him.

"May I kiss the bride?" Seth asked, his voice low and unexpectedly shy.

"You'd better," Brenda quipped, her sass momentarily veiling her nerves. But as his lips met hers, a flutter of laughter escaped her, softening into something sweet.

They stepped apart, faces flushed with more than the Texan heat. There was relief, yes, but also a shared sense of purpose. They were in this together now, bound not just by words, but by a joint commitment to see it through.

"Ready to start?" Seth asked, his hand finding hers once more.

"Let's build something," Brenda agreed, and the simplicity of the statement was their promise to each other.

Chapter Five

B renda couldn't help the flutter in her stomach as Seth Clinkinbeard pulled his horse to a stop in front of the sprawling ranch. It was dark and all she could do to see anything, but the house in front of her looked large. Large enough for all the children she could want. She dismounted from the back of Seth's horse and she took a deep breath to steady herself. Now that she was actually married, she couldn't help but wonder if she'd lost her mind agreeing to marry a stranger.

"Quite the place you have here," Brenda said. She brushed a stray blond lock from her face, hoping her tone conveyed more confidence than she felt. "Must be a lot of work running it all."

Seth's lips quirked up at the edges. "It is, but I wouldn't have it any other way," he replied.

Brenda followed him toward the main house, taking in the worn wooden planks and the porch that wrapped around the front. A sense of purpose filled her chest. "I'd like to learn, you know. About ranching." Her words tumbled out, eager and earnest.

"Would you?" There was a hint of surprise in Seth's tone, and he glanced over at her.

"Sure." Brenda nodded, her spirit undampened by his brief silence. "Never been one to shy away from getting my hands dirty. Plus, I think it's better than spending my days talking to the chickens and waiting for the walls to answer back."

"Is that so?" Seth's mouth twitched again, this time a smile threatening to break free. He led her up the steps, his stride confident and sure. "You know part of your day will need to be spent cooking, cleaning, and doing all those things wives do."

"Absolutely," Brenda affirmed, following close on his heels. "And don't worry about me keeping up. I'm quick on the uptake, and I've got a knack for...well, most things." She let out a soft chuckle. "Except maybe singing. I've even had small children cover their ears and run for the hills when I start singing."

"Most things, huh?" Seth's voice carried a note of amusement, and when he looked back at her, there was a warmth in his eyes she hadn't seen before.

"Except cooking," Brenda added quickly. "Well, I'm a decent cook, but I don't much care for it."

"Guess we'll see about that," Seth said, opening the door to the house for her, the flicker of a challenge in his gaze.

"Guess we will," Brenda agreed.

He stepped closer, and she could feel the heat of his body even before his lips met hers.

"Wha—" Brenda started, but the question was swept away by the sudden rush of the moment. She'd meant to learn about the ranch, but this was the kind of learning she should have on her wedding night. His kiss, hesitant at first, grew more confident, mirroring the boldness that often characterized her own spirit.

They stumbled as they kissed and stroked and learned each other. With a bashful yet earnest clumsiness, they found their way to Seth's bedroom, leaving the world behind.

The room was simple, the bed unadorned, but none of that mattered as they made love for the first time. It was a mix of awkward pauses and soft laughter. Every touch was a revelation.

Afterward, Brenda lay beside Seth, her skin still tingling from their shared experience. She turned her head, watching him as his breathing slowed and deep sleep claimed him. She wanted to talk, to get to know him better and talk about shared dreams for their future. But he was asleep, and she was left alone with her thoughts.

She stared up at the ceiling. Her heart was a tangle of emotions—joy, yearning, a touch of uncertainty. Her life had been a series of moments leading to this, and she still clung to the hope of sunshine, unicorns, and rainbows.

"Tomorrow," she whispered to the quiet room, "we'll find our way."

BEFORE THE SUN WAS up the following day, Brenda rolled out of bed, her feet hitting the cool wooden floorboards with a silent determination. She tiptoed through the stillness of the ranch house, determined to start the day right. Seth's slumbering form remained undisturbed as she left their room behind.

In the kitchen, she wrestled with the cast-iron skillet, her blond hair tied back in a hasty knot. Cooking had never been her favorite thing, but for Seth, she'd try her hand at anything. The eggs sizzled as she scrambled them, and she hummed a tune under her breath—a hopeful melody for what lay ahead.

"Morning," Seth grumbled, shuffling into the kitchen just as Brenda placed two simple plates on the worn table.

"Morning," she replied, her smile as bright as the dawn light spilling through the window. "I hope you like your eggs this way."

He nodded, his eyes half-closed, and forked a mouthful of eggs without much ado. Brenda watched him for a moment, her heart skipping with a mixture of affection and anticipation. "So," she said, eager to bridge the silence between them, "I can't wait to see all there is to the ranch. It must be quite the operation to keep running smoothly."

"Yep," Seth said between bites, his attention more on his plate than on her words.

"Is there...I mean, maybe later, could you show me around?" Brenda asked.

"Maybe," he muttered, already standing up with his plate cleared. "Got lots to do today. Calves won't brand themselves."

"Oh, of course." Brenda's smile didn't quite reach her eyes as she watched him rinse his plate and head for the door. "Well, have a good day."

"Uh-huh," Seth said over his shoulder, grabbing his hat from its peg and stepping out into the growing light.

Brenda sat at the table long after he'd gone, her breakfast cold and forgotten. The house felt huge and empty, a stark contrast to the noisy warmth of the orphanage she once called home. She had dreamt of laughter echoing through these walls, of shared smiles over morning coffee. But the silence was heavy, a blanket that smothered her romantic notions.

She pushed her plate away, her green eyes clouding with disappointment. This wasn't the companionship she'd envisioned—this wasn't the partnership of dreams. Where were the unicorns and rainbows she had so naively believed in? The love that was supposed to light up even the darkest corners?

"Darn it, Brenda," she scolded herself softly, "you're not one to mope."

But as she stood and began to clear the table, her actions robotic and efficient, there was no denying the growing ache in her chest.

"I guess I'd better milk the cows and gather eggs," she whispered. "We'll find our way. We have to."

Brenda carried the pail of milk inside and looked around the dusty kitchen. The sun outside cast long beams across the wooden floor, highlighting every speck of dirt and stray crumb. With a determined glint in her green eyes, she grabbed the broom and began sweeping with vigor. She imagined each stroke as a step closer to making this house – this life – her own.

After a thorough scrubbing of the kitchen that left her arms aching and her brow beaded with sweat, Brenda moved on to the parlor. She attacked the task with the same fervor, fluffing pillows and dusting off surfaces until the room took on a more welcoming air.

"Wouldn't hurt to have a bit of charm around here," she said, eyeing her handiwork. It was far from the grandeur of the mansion in Beckham, Massachusetts, where she had worked, but it was becoming hers, piece by piece.

With lunchtime approaching, Brenda went back into the kitchen, tying on an apron that hung from a hook by the door. She decided to fix sandwiches, something simple yet satisfying, hoping they would provide an opportunity for conversation.

"Let's see if cowboy appetites are as big as their boots," she said, arranging the plates just so on the table.

The clock ticked away the minutes, and as high noon came and went, Brenda's initial enthusiasm waned. She waited, staring out the window. It was beautiful, yes, but after just a few hours, the isolation gnawed at her. There were no neighbors stopping by for tea, no chatter of children playing – just the unyielding silence of the prairie.

"Big sky, big dreams, and even bigger loneliness," she sighed, crossing her arms as she leaned against the windowsill.

Finally, the sound of boots thudding on the porch pulled her from her reverie. Seth entered, his hat in hand, and Brenda's heart leaped despite her resolve.

"Made us lunch," she announced with forced cheerfulness. "Hope you're hungry."

"Starving," Seth replied with a nod, though his eyes barely met hers.

They sat together, the sounds of chewing and clinking silverware filling the room.

Brenda's bright smile and animated gestures as she recounted the story of the chickens' antics. Seth's expression remained stoic, contrasting sharply with Brenda's attempts at levity.

Seth didn't even smile. "Chickens need to be fenced better," he stated flatly.

"Right, of course," Brenda agreed. "I'll remember that."

As Seth stood to leave, Brenda's voice caught him at the door. "Maybe tonight we can...talk?"

"Got work to do," Seth said, shrugging on his dusty coat. "But thanks for lunch."

And with that, he was gone, leaving Brenda alone with her thoughts and the echo of her own voice in the empty house. Her determination didn't falter, but as she cleared the table, she couldn't help but wonder how many more meals she could carry on a one-sided conversation without losing her mind.

BRENDA STOOD BY THE window, watching as Seth mended a fence out in the pasture. With a sigh, she turned away and busied herself with tidying up what was already immaculate. The ranch house might be dust-free, but her heart felt coated with the weight of silence.

"Need any help with that?" she called out when Seth finally trudged back toward the house hours later, his shirt sticking to his back.

Seth paused, squinting against the sunlight's glare, then shook his head. "Nope. You're doing fine, Brenda."

"Fine," she said, feeling frustrated. "I meant outside, with the ranch work."

"Ah." He took off his hat and wiped his brow with a forearm. "It's tough work, not really suited for—"

"Me?" she interjected, crossing her arms. It wasn't a question. "I'm stronger than I look, you know."

"Sure," Seth nodded, though his tone was dismissive. "But it's best you keep to the house, Brenda. That's plenty."

"Plenty lonely, you mean," she muttered under her breath, turning to shuffle some utensils on the counter that didn't need shuffling.

"Something you said?" Seth asked, reaching for the water pitcher.

"Actually, yes." Brenda turned to face him, her green eyes fixed upon his with a daring that defied her soft exterior. "I said it's lonely. This place, it's so quiet you can hear your own heartbeat. I thought, maybe, we could work together sometimes. Or at least...talk more."

"Talk?" Seth seemed genuinely puzzled. "We talk plenty."

"About chickens and fences," Brenda pressed, her voice steadier than she felt. "Not about us."

"Us?"

"Never mind." She waved a hand, dismissing both the topic and the swell of disappointment.

"Look, Brenda," Seth said, setting down the empty pitcher, his gaze sliding past hers. "We agreed to this marriage because it made sense, right? You needed a home, and I needed help around here. There's no use complicating things."

"Complicating," she said. "Right."

"Exactly." He nodded, satisfied, missing the bite in her tone. "Glad we understand each other."

She watched him walk away. In the wake of his departure, she allowed herself a moment to lean against the cool wood of the kitchen table. Her dreams of love and companionship felt like foolish girlhood fantasies against the stark reality of a husband who saw her as part of the ranch's inventory—a useful asset, nothing more.

Brenda lifted her chin, the set of her jaw firm. She wouldn't cry. There was no room for tears on a ranch. Instead, she'd find a way to bridge the gap or build a life rich enough that it wouldn't matter. But deep down, she couldn't quench the hope for something more—a sign that beyond the endless fields and silent meals, there lay a promise of rainbows.

BRENDA SLIPPED OUT the back door, the heavy silence of the ranch house pressing down on her like the heat of the Texas sun. She made her way to the stables, the soft murmur of animals growing louder as she approached. The barn was a world away from the quiet indifference of the house, pulsing with the simple, honest life of creatures who didn't mask their feelings.

"Hey there," Brenda cooed, her fingers trailing along the rough wood of the stalls. A nicker of greeting met her from Daisy, the palomino mare. Brenda's hands found their way into Daisy's mane, the horse leaning into the touch with a gentleness that filled a hollow space in Brenda's chest.

"Who needs words when you've got this?" Brenda asked. In these moments, she could almost forget the gnawing loneliness.

Seth leaned against the fence of the corral, watching Brenda from a distance. He'd come looking for a tool he'd left behind but found himself observing her instead. He could hear her laugh and he smiled at the sound.

Seth rubbed the back of his neck, frustration knotting between his shoulder blades. He wasn't blind. He could see she was unhappy. It nagged at him, the realization that maybe, he hadn't considered her needs in their marriage.

"Everything all right out here?" he asked, wishing he knew exactly what was wrong and how to fix it.

Brenda straightened up, brushing stray strands of hair from her face. "Just fine, Seth. Daisy here's been keeping me company."

"Good...good." Seth cleared his throat. "Animals are easy to please, at least."

"Sometimes easier than people," she replied with a pointed look.

"Suppose that's true." He shoved his hands into his pockets, the leather gloves crumpling with the motion. Silence stretched between them.

"Guess I better get back to it," Seth finally mumbled, retreating to the safety of work and routine.

"Sure, Seth." Brenda watched him go.

BRENDA'S HANDS MOVED deftly, kneading dough. She hummed an old tune, one remembered from her days in the orphanage, happy there was no one around to tell her to stop. This was her domain now, and she took pride in the tangible evidence of her labors—a loaf of bread, a swept floor, linens drying crisp and white in the summer heat.

"Sure smells good in here," she muttered to herself.

Yet as she stepped back to admire her handiwork, Brenda's thoughts drifted. The silence of the house seemed louder than usual, and the weight of solitude pressed against her chest. She thought of Seth—out there somewhere on the vast expanse of land, tending to cattle or mending fences—anywhere but here with her.

"Should be enough for two," she whispered to the empty room. She glanced at the clock. Lunchtime was nearing, but would he come? Every day she made lunch for him, and he only showed up to eat it about half the time.

"Can't force someone to talk if they don't want to," she said aloud. She looked out the window, scanning the horizon for a sign of him. The bread would be done soon, perfect and warm. Maybe the way to a man's heart really was through his stomach.

"Got to give it time," she reassured herself. Would time be enough to turn a marriage of convenience into something real, something that resembled the companionship she craved?

Brenda pulled the bread out of the oven, setting it on the counter with a satisfied sigh. She'd keep trying, keep hoping. After all, wasn't hope what had brought her to this sprawling Texas ranch in the first place?

BRENDA WIPED THE SWEAT from her brow with the back of her hand. Her steps carried her with purpose across the yard to where Seth was repairing a fence, his back to her.

"Hey, Seth," she called out, her voice steady despite the butterflies dancing in her stomach. He turned a nail between his lips, squinting against the sunlight.

"Need something?" His words were muffled, and he pulled the nail from his mouth.

Brenda took a deep breath, the scent of freshly cut hay mingling with her determination. "We need to talk. About us."

"Us?" The word seemed foreign on his lips.

"Yes, us." Brenda planted her feet firmly. "I came here to be your wife, not just a shadow in your house who cooks and cleans for you. I want...no, I need more from this marriage."

Seth glared at her for a moment, but Brenda wasn't one to back down. "You mean you want more talking? More...feelings?"

"Exactly. It's not just about work and keeping the ranch going. There has to be more between us," she insisted.

"Feelings don't mend fences or manage cattle," Seth replied. "Look, I know you're looking for someone to talk to, but we'll go to church tomorrow, and you'll get to see all your friends. Or would you call them sisters?"

"I call them sisters," Brenda said. "Having friends, family, people you love. They make life worth living. Being alone all the time is not something I should be required to do."

"You'll be able to start visiting with your sisters. I know it feels like you're isolated, but once you learn where they all live, you can walk to see them, or even ride. Up to you."

"That's all good and well, but I want to talk to my husband."

Seth regarded her for a long moment. Finally, he sighed. "All right. We'll talk. After supper?"

"Thank you, Seth. That's all I'm asking for." Brenda's heart fluttered with hope.

Turning on her heel, she headed back to the house, her mind already racing with plans for supper. She wanted to cook something special. Then they would talk.

Chapter Six

Seth Clinkinbeard shifted uneasily on the wooden pew, his gaze darting between the preacher and the exit. As soon as the service ended, he made a beeline for David Dailey, who was shaking hands with fellow parishioners outside the church.

"David," Seth called out.

"Morning, Seth. Something on your mind?" David asked.

Seth ran a hand through his hair, a telltale sign of frustration. "It's Brenda," he began. "She thinks I ought to be doting on her every hour of every day."

David shielded his eyes from the bright Texas sun. "A woman needs to feel connected to her man, Seth. More than just...in the bedroom."

Seth's brow creased. "But we're together every night. Thought that'd be enough."

"Intimacy is more than what happens after dark, my friend," David said, a knowing look crossing his weathered face. "Why don't you take a day off? Sundays are good for resting and courting your wife."

"Court Brenda?" Seth snorted at the thought. "I don't have time for courting. There's work to be done. Besides, she's already my wife. Why would I need to court her?"

"Take a day, Seth. Take her for a drive, talk to her, listen. It'll do you both some good," David suggested with a gentle firmness.

Seth pondered for a moment. "All right," he conceded with a reluctant nod. "I suppose a drive after lunch wouldn't hurt."

"Good man," David clapped Seth on the shoulder, a smile spreading across his face. "You might find you enjoy it more than you think."

The church bells had long stopped ringing by the time Seth and Brenda headed out for a drive that afternoon. "Thought you could use some fresh air," Seth said, feeling a bit out of place trying to court his wife.

"I sure could." A drive was the last thing she expected. "Well, I suppose I could do with a change of scenery." He'd promised to talk with her the night before, but they'd exchanged a few words before he was dragging her to the bedroom, and as always, he fell asleep right after.

"Nice day for it," Seth remarked, his hands firm on the leads.

"Sure is," Brenda said.

Seth cleared his throat, breaking the comfortable silence. "Been thinking about the ranch," he said, squinting into the horizon. "Got plans, big ones. More cattle, maybe some more land. Our neighbors to the north have too much land for them. Husband's getting older, and they don't have children."

"Sounds ambitious," she said, watching a hawk circle lazily above them.

"Yep. And there's the matter of inheritance. Ranch needs a son, someone to carry on the Clinkinbeard name." He glanced at her sideways, a seriousness creasing his brow.

Brenda felt a twinge of something—was it annoyance or hurt?—but she kept her voice even. "A son," she repeated.

"Thought you'd be glad to hear it. It's important, Brenda. You understand that, don't you?" His gaze was earnest.

"Of course, I understand," she replied, forcing a smile though her mind raced with thoughts unvoiced.

BRENDA HEAVED THE WINDOW open, hoping for relief from the heat. She could almost hear the laughter of her sisters on the wind—a sound she longed for.

"I have never been this hot in my life," she muttered to herself, fanning her face with the hem of her apron.

The idea popped into her head like a firefly flickering to life in the dark expanse of her discontent. She would invite the girls over, her sisters. A gathering would be just the remedy to her unsettled spirits.

She fetched the writing paper and penned quick notes to each of them. "Afternoon tea and cookies at my home tomorrow," it read. "Come for laughter and sisterhood." She knew they'd come. They always stood by one another, no matter the distance or dust between them.

She went out and saddled the gelding Seth had told her was the calmest, and she rode to each of their homes, having gotten directions from them at church on Sunday. All of them, except Amy, agreed to come. Amy was going to town with her stepdaughters that afternoon to buy fabric for new dresses. She'd talk to Amy at another time.

As Brenda prepared the dough for the cookies, she couldn't help but replay Seth's words about needing a son. Annoyance bubbled inside. To be seen as nothing more than someone to bear his children—it pricked at her pride.

"Talking to me like I'm some broodmare," she grumbled. But within the layers of her irritation, a small, silvery thread of comfort weaved through her thoughts. He was talking, after all—sharing plans, thoughts, a bit of himself. It wasn't much, but it was a start.

"Maybe this afternoon, with the girls around, I'll find a way to see it clearer," she mused. "Or at least laugh enough to forget for a spell."

With the last cookie placed on the tray, Brenda peered out the window again, her heart aflutter with the promise of company and connection. She couldn't wait for her sisters to arrive.

Brenda arranged a circle of chairs in the parlor. A pitcher of iced tea was on the table, next to a plate stacked with cookies.

"Look at you, all domestic," teased Imogene, the youngest, her eyes twinkling as she hugged Brenda.

Once settled, Brenda took a deep breath. "I really need my sisters." She fidgeted with her apron, gathering the courage to voice her heart's troubles.

"Spill it, Brenda," urged Cassandra.

"It's Seth," Brenda said. "He talks plans for the ranch, about needing a son to pass it all to, but he doesn't see me. Not really."

"Men can be blind," said Deborah.

"Doesn't mean they don't care," added Cassandra, reaching across to squeeze Brenda's hand.

"Maybe so, but I feel more like part of the furniture than his wife. Where's the laughter, the...connection? It's all duty and no heart."

"Have you told him this?" Erna asked, her brow furrowed with concern.

"Can't find the words," Brenda admitted.

"Start simple," suggested Faith. "Tell him how you're feeling, not just what you're doing."

"Compromise, too," Cassandra said. "Find something you both enjoy, make it your thing."

"And don't forget the listening part," Gail said. "It goes both ways."

"True enough," Brenda conceded, feeling the knot in her chest loosen just a bit. "And I suppose there's no harm in trying to draw him out some."

"Exactly!" her sisters exclaimed in unison, their laughter ringing through the room.

"All right then," Brenda said, a spark igniting in her gaze. "I'll give it a shot. After all, what's marriage but a dance of give and take?"

Nods of agreement circled around as the conversation flowed into the late afternoon, the room filled with stories, advice, and the comforting presence of family. Brenda listened, laughed, and learned, feeling a great deal more hopeful as she was surrounded by her sisters.

Brenda sat on the porch swing, her sisters around her. The wooden boards creaked softly under their collective weight, the rhythm a soothing backdrop to their conversation.

"Remember, Brenda," said Hannah, her voice gentle, "you're worth more than you think. Don't let him forget that."

"Speak your heart to Seth." Cassandra leaned forward, urging her sister to do what she thought was best.

"I guess I will," Brenda said. "Just need to find the right words."

"Keep it simple," Hannah suggested.

When Brenda went to bed that night, she was still trying to find the right words to talk to Seth. She lay awake long after they'd made love, and he was snoring beside her, trying to figure out just what to do to make their marriage work.

A loud rapping on the door startled her, but she jumped out of bed and pulled a dress over her head, not bothering to button the back. She'd take care of that later.

She knew it was probably just one of the ranch hands with an emergency for Seth, but he wasn't awake, and she was. Therefore, she would go to the door.

Tim Stockwell, his hat clutched in one hand, stood in the doorway. His face was drawn, eyes reflecting worry that cut straight to Brenda's core.

"It's Amy," he said, the tremble in his voice betraying his stoic appearance. "She's got a terrible fever."

"I'm coming," Brenda said, hurrying back into the house.

Dressed in practical attire, Brenda grabbed her medicinal bag— a collection of remedies and tonics she'd learned to trust. She glanced back at Tim, their faces illuminated by concern and lamplight.

Brenda stepped out into the night, following Tim who hadn't bothered to hitch up the wagon when he found his wife so ill.

For two weeks, Brenda remained at Amy's side, nursing her through fevers and coughing fits. She became a fixture in the dimly lit room, where whispers of recovery slowly began to mingle with the lingering traces of illness.

When all of the sisters came to help, Brenda easily put them to work. They all had unique skills, and Amy was the oldest among them...the one who had done the most for them.

SETH STOOD IN THE MIDDLE of the kitchen, a pan in one hand and an egg hovering precariously over it. Seth sighed, reluctantly acknowledging that Brenda's absence was more than just an inconvenience.

"Doggonit," he muttered under his breath, reaching for a cloth to wipe up the mess. Each day without her seemed longer than the last.

For two weeks, Seth's routine went back to what it was before Brenda had come into his life. The bed remained unmade, the sheets tangled from his restless sleep. He wasn't sure which he missed more: Brenda's cooking or her company.

She had taken care of him in a way he hadn't realized he'd needed. It was nice not to eat with the other men and have a pretty woman to look at. The house was getting dirty again.

It was strange how quiet the house felt. He'd sit on the porch after sundown, staring out at the expanse of his land, feeling an emptiness . Her laughter, her sharp-witted remarks, even her sass – he yearned for all of it.

"Never thought I'd miss someone talking back to me," he confessed to the silent stars.

When Brenda finally returned, dusty from the trail, her hair tousled from the wind, Seth's heart skipped a beat. She looked weary but strong, her green eyes reflecting a depth he'd previously overlooked.

"Welcome home, Brenda," he said, voice gentle as he took her bag.

"Thanks, Seth. Amy's better now," she replied, her voice hoarse from exhaustion.

"Let's sit down," he suggested, leading her to the sofa. Brenda sank into the cushions, watching him with a mixture of curiosity and fatigue.

"I've missed you," Seth started, fumbling for words that didn't come naturally. "Not just for the cooking and the cleaning. I missed you, Brenda. Just you."

She raised an eyebrow, taken aback by his admission. "Really?"

"Really," he said, taking her hands in his. "I've been a fool. You're more than I ever expected, and I promise things will be better. I'll listen more, be there for you, not just when we...well, you know."

A smile tugged at the corner of Brenda's lips. "And Sundays off?"

"Every single one," he vowed, a hopeful glint in his eye.

"All right then," Brenda said, allowing herself to lean into his embrace. His admission of missing her had been unexpected, but welcome. It was good that he realized she was there...finally.

When he kissed her, she responded to him eagerly. The one thing she loved more than anything about being married to Seth was their time in bed together. And she'd missed him.

Chapter Seven

Seth spent the next two weeks being a persistent suitor. Brenda observed with amusement as he tried his hand at courting.

"Brenda," he began on one sweltering afternoon, leaning against the fence while she tended to the garden, "I reckon a lady like yourself could use a break. Perhaps a ride out to the creek?"

Brenda wiped her brow, casting a skeptical glance his way. "Mr. Clinkinbeard, do you even know how to relax by a creek? You strike me as the sort to bring a hammer and nails to a picnic, so you can build a fence around the area."

He chuckled, a bit sheepishly. "Well, I might need some teaching on leisure, I suppose."

She smiled gently at his attempt, recognizing the effort behind it. And so, for two weeks, Seth persistently showed up with small offerings—a wildflower bouquet, an invitation to the church social, a promise of a special dinner under the stars. Each gesture was simple, earnest, and increasingly endearing.

However, as the days rolled on, the old Seth began to resurface. It started subtly with just a missed supper here, a forgotten walk there—all excused by urgent matters at the ranch. The rhythm of their newfound companionship stumbled, faltered, and soon Brenda found herself once more second to Seth's first love: his work.

"Got to mend the fences before the cattle stray," Seth called out early one morning, already saddled up and halfway out the door.

"Of course," Brenda replied, trying to hide the disappointment in her voice. "The fences can't wait, I understand."

"Appreciate it, Brenda," he said with a tip of his hat before disappearing into the growing light of dawn.

As the hours passed, Brenda sat on the porch, her eyes watching the horizon where Seth had vanished. She sipped her tea, the silence around her speaking volumes. Once again, she was alone, the brief interlude of courtship seeming more like a dream than a memory.

BRENDA'S FINGERS TRAILED along the fabric of her new dress, a cascade of cornflower blue that made her green eyes shimmer. Cassandra had outdone herself. Every stitch was placed with care, every pleat and hem designed to flatter.

"Feels like wearing a cloud, doesn't it?" Cassandra said, her voice tinged with pride. She stood back, admiring her handiwork.

"Like a dream," Brenda confessed, turning this way and that before the looking glass. "But will Seth even notice?"

Cassandra tucked a stray blond lock behind Brenda's ear. "If he doesn't, he's blinder than a bat."

Brenda laughed the sound light as the airy fabric hugging her form. "Let's hope for a miracle then."

"Girl, you don't need miracles. You just be you," Cassandra encouraged, her eyes sparkling with sisterly affection.

That evening, Brenda stood in the kitchen, sleeves rolled up over her elbows as she tackled a special meal. The table was set with flowers, and Brenda had managed to cook up a roast with all the trimmings—a feat for a woman who claimed an aversion to culinary pursuits.

"Smells good in here," Seth remarked as he stepped into the house, his gaze fixed on the papers in his hand.

"Thank you," Brenda replied, hoping to catch his attention. "Thought we could have a nice supper."

"Sounds great." Seth barely glanced up, missing the sight of Brenda dressed up for him.

They ate mostly in silence. Brenda tried to engage Seth in conversation, but his replies were brief, distracted. As soon as the last bite was swallowed, Seth pushed back his chair.

"Got to fix a stall in the barn," he mumbled, standing up. "Thanks for supper, Brenda."

"Sure," she replied, her voice tinged with disappointment. She watched through the window as Seth walked away from the house.

The new dress lost its luster as the evening wore on, and Brenda cleared the plates, the heaviness in her heart a stark contrast to the optimism that had filled the room only hours before.

BRENDA SAT ALONE IN the dimly lit parlor, the last embers of the fire casting a weak glow across her tear-streaked face. She had tried, truly tried, to get Seth to notice her, to be more than just a convenient fixture in his life.

She let out a soft sob, one hand clutching the fabric of her dress—a dress that had promised so much but delivered so little. Then, with a sniff and a determined set to her jaw, Brenda stood up. "Enough is enough," she whispered to herself. Her spirit, usually so bright and unyielding, refused to wilt under neglect.

With quiet resolve, she climbed the staircase. She bypassed the master bedroom—Seth's room—and instead opened the door to a smaller, unused room. It was plain, with a modest bed and a small window that looked out over the prairie. It would do.

She didn't bother with a nightgown. Instead, she lay atop the covers, still wearing her new dress.

Meanwhile, Seth worked on the stubborn stall door, the sound of hammer meeting nail a steady rhythm in the night. His mind raced with numbers, plans for expansion, cattle prices—but not once did it brush upon the thought of Brenda waiting at home.

It was only when he was so tired he could barely see straight that he stowed away his tools and made his way back to the house, a tired yawn escaping him as he stepped through the back door.

"Supper sure did hit the spot," he called out, half-expecting Brenda to emerge from the kitchen with a tart reply ready on her lips. Silence greeted him. He frowned, the annoyance creeping in as he navigated the familiar rooms. "Brenda?"

No answer.

He checked the parlor, the lingering scent of their meal still hanging in the air. Not there. The master bedroom, too, was vacant, its bed untouched. He scratched his head, irritation mounting. Where could she be?

"Probably fussing over some stray cat or other," he grumbled, too weary to muster the energy for a proper search. A vague sense of unease tugged at him, but exhaustion won out. With a shrug, he surrendered to sleep.

BRENDA WAS UP BEFORE the sun as usual the following morning. She made breakfast with her usual care, when all she really wanted to do was fling the eggs she was making at her husband's head.

Seth sat down at the breakfast table as she put their plates down, and he immediately tucked into his food. "You were missing last night," he said, not looking up.

"I was missing because I'm sick of being an afterthought. Sick of you treating me like another possession. I am a person with feelings, Seth," Brenda's voice was filled with anger. "I am not just someone you can put on a shelf and dust off when it's convenient for you. I'm your wife, and I deserve more than the scraps of your attention."

Seth finally looked up, his expression a mixture of surprise and realization. "I have work!"

Brenda held his gaze steadily, her green eyes flashing with the fire of her emotions. "I understand you have work, Seth. But I am not asking to be your first priority every moment of the day. I'm asking for respect, a kind word, a moment of genuine connection that doesn't revolve around fixing fences or mending stalls."

Seth's brow furrowed as he processed her words. For the first time, he saw the hurt and loneliness in Brenda's eyes.

"I didn't mean to make you feel that way," Seth said, his voice softer than she had heard in a long time. "I've been so caught up in trying to keep everything running smoothly here at the ranch that I forgot to take care of what truly matters."

Brenda felt a flicker of hope ignite within her as she listened to Seth's earnest words. Perhaps there was a chance for them after all.

"It's not just about the ranch, Seth," Brenda said, her voice gentler now. "It's about us, about our marriage. I want us to be a team, partners in this life we've built together."

Seth nodded. "You're right, Brenda. I'm going to do better. I promise."

Brenda's heart swelled with both relief and affection as she reached out to clasp Seth's hand across the table. "Thank you." It felt good for him to even acknowledge how she felt. She'd reserve the egg throwing for later, but she certainly wasn't above it.

BRENDA SET ABOUT HER work, a determined glint in her eyes. She moved with purpose around the yard of her modest homestead, tying colorful ribbons to the branches of the old oak tree and setting up tables groaning under the weight of potato salad, cornbread, and jars of sweet tea.

"It's so hot," she muttered, wiping sweat from her brow with the back of her hand.

"Looks wonderful," chuckled her sister Amy, stepping into the yard with a basket of freshly picked peaches. Her husband, Tim, followed close behind, already strumming his guitar, filling the air with the lazy notes of a familiar tune.

"Where's Seth?" Amy asked, glancing around the bustling space.

"Off mending stalls or fences or dealing with an injured hoof. Where else?" Brenda replied, a touch sharper than intended. She took a deep breath, plastering on a smile. "But today's not about him—it's about family."

"Mrs. Hackenschleimer sent pie!" Susan called as she and David walked through the open gate, arms laden with blankets and more food. They settled in quickly, laughter and chattering rising above the clink of ice in glasses and the sizzle of meat cooked outside.

"David, do you think you could find Seth for supper?" Brenda asked, her tone light but her request clear.

"Sure thing," David said with an easy smile, nodding toward Amos, who had just arrived. "Pastor, care to join me?"

"Of course," Amos replied, his gentle eyes crinkling at the corners as he smiled. He touched Hannah's arm before walking away with David.

Together, they made their way to the barn where Seth was holed up, hammering away.

"Evening, Seth," David greeted, leaning against the door frame. "Brenda's whipped up a feast fit for kings, and there's dancing to be had after. You wouldn't want to miss it."

"Supper can wait," Seth grunted, not looking up from his work. "This stall won't fix itself."

"The work of our hands is important," Amos chimed in, his voice soft yet firm. "But so is the work of our hearts. Come, your wife has put in too much work planning this evening and getting everything ready. It would be rude for you to be late."

Seth paused, considering the pastor's words. He wiped his brow and finally met their gazes. There was something in the way Amos looked at him—a quiet understanding—that nudged at Seth's conscience.

"All right," Seth conceded, setting down his tools. "Just give me a minute to wash up."

As he walked past David and Amos, the faint sound of laughter drew him in, the warmth of the gathering calling to something deep inside him that he hadn't realized was yearning for connection.

"Seems like a mighty fine evening," Seth admitted, almost to himself, as he glimpsed Brenda through the window, her laughter mingling with the golden hues of the setting sun.

Later, Seth stood with a group of his friends, all sharing a laugh about a story Tim told about his daughters.

"Say, Seth," Aaron, one of his new brothers-in-law said, his chuckle fading into concern. "You think Brenda's all right with how much time you spend working? She seems a little put out with you tonight."

"Course she's all right with it," Seth replied, a tad too quickly. "Why wouldn't she be?"

"Women need attention, Seth," Joel said. "And Brenda, she's a gem. She was there for Tim and Amy when they needed her. All the girls talk about what a good person Brenda is."

Seth shifted uncomfortably. He had been more interested in the ranch than his new wife. But wasn't that what a man was supposed to do? Provide?

"Look here," said Tim, taking a step closer to Seth. "Brenda's not just any woman. She's got spirit, that one. And if you don't pay attention to her, you're gonna lose her."

"Tim's right," Amos added, nodding. "We've seen how she looks at you, like you hung the moon and stars. But lately...well, those stares look more like she wants to throw a brick at your head."

"Aw, come on," Seth protested, though doubt niggled at his heart. "She knows I have work—"

"Work can wait," Andrew cut in, holding up a hand. "A good woman won't. She made you supper, dressed up nice, and you walked right past her. That's no way to treat a lady." He shook his head. "Cassandra told me that she made her a pretty dress, and you didn't even notice, and didn't talk to her. Instead, you went out to the barn to work. She said Brenda cried to her about it the next day."

"I've heard stories about Brenda when she's angry," Aaron said with a wry grin. "I hear she has a sharp tongue and a temper to match."

"Being present ain't about being in the room, Seth," Tim said softly, placing a hand on Seth's shoulder. "It's about being there for her."

"Besides," Max piped in, "if she leaves, who's gonna put up with your grumpy mug every morning?"

Their words stung, but Seth knew they came from a place of love—just like everything in this tight-knit community. He watched as Brenda laughed with her sisters.

"All right," Seth conceded after a long moment, a small smile breaking through his stubbornness. "I get what y'all are saying. I'll try harder."

"Good man," Tim said, patting his back as they all turned to join the festivities.

LATER, AFTER ALMOST everyone had left, Seth leaned against the porch railing, his gaze lingering on his wife, who was talking to Amy.

"Guess I've been looking but not really seeing," Seth murmured to himself.

"Seeing what?" Tim's voice drifted from behind him, as he stepped out onto the porch.

Seth turned, the wooden planks creaking under his boots. "Brenda," he said simply.

"Ah." Tim nodded, understanding written plain on his face. "You going to do something about it?"

"Yup. I reckon I owe her more than I've given."

"Good. She deserves your time, Seth. More than the ranch does."

"Can't argue with that." Seth looked away. "I tried, you know? A while back. Took her out for walks, even tried my hand at dancing. But then...the ranch needed me."

"Seems to me," Tim said, tipping his hat back, "the ranch will always need you. But Brenda, she might not always wait around."

"Right again." Seth's jaw clenched as he faced the truth that had been gnawing at him. He had let the land, the cattle, and the endless work overshadow the woman who'd come into his life like a breath of fresh air on a muggy Texas day.

"Tomorrow," Seth declared with newfound resolve, "I'm starting fresh. I need to show her she's my priority."

"Better late than never," Tim agreed with a chuckle.

Chapter Eight

Seth wiped the sweat from his brow as he dug his shovel into the earth. Brenda knelt beside him, her hands deep in the dirt as she planted peas. The sun bore down on them. "Why is it so hot still?" Brenda asked. "It's halfway through September!"

Seth smiled. "Spoken like a true Yankee. You're in Texas now."

"Pass me that watering can, would you?" Brenda asked without looking up, knowing Seth would have it ready.

"Here you go," he responded, handing it over.

"Looks like we'll have a good harvest at this rate," she remarked. The idea of planting in late September was foreign to her, but she'd heard there were plants that would be fine, so she was going to try it.

"Thanks to your green thumb," Seth acknowledged. "These plants are fairing better than I would've managed alone." He laughed. "Not that I kept a kitchen garden before you got here. I just ate with the men."

Brenda shrugged lightly. "We all have our strengths. Yours is making sure this place doesn't fall apart."

"Speaking of which," Brenda said, brushing a strand of hair from her face, "Mrs. Dailey mentioned there's a church social this evening. Thought it might be nice to attend, see some friendly faces."

Seth's hand paused mid-dig. He glanced up at her, the idea not quite aligning with his vision of an ideal evening. "A social, huh?"

"Come on, it'll be fun. Besides, we could use a break from the ranch." Her green eyes sparkled with mischief. "And I hear Amy baked four pies for the occasion."

He chuckled, knowing full well Brenda's penchant for pie. "I suppose we could spare a few hours."

"Is that a 'yes' I hear, Mr. Clinkinbeard?" She arched an eyebrow playfully.

"All right," Seth conceded with a mock sigh, standing and dusting off his hands. "You win. Let's go to that social."

Brenda's smile bloomed like the flowers around them. "Great! It's settled then." It had been all she could do to convince him to spend the day helping her in the garden, and now he was agreeing to a social. She couldn't wait. He certainly was trying, and she appreciated that.

"Anything to see you smile," he murmured.

BRENDA STOOD BEFORE her mirror, fiddling with the collar of her blouse. The fabric was simple, but clean and carefully pressed—an effort not lost on her as she carefully swept her hair up into a new style Cassandra had shown her.

"Could you help me with this?" she called out, struggling with a hairpin that seemed to have a mind of its own.

Seth appeared in the doorway, his usual work attire replaced by a clean white shirt and suspenders that accentuated his broad shoulders. "Let me see," he said.

"Never figured you for a man who could handle hairpins," Brenda teased, suppressing a smile as Seth's fingers worked surprisingly deftly at her hair.

"Got plenty of practice helping my sister before she got married and moved away," Seth admitted. "There. That should hold."

"Thanks." Brenda flashed him a grateful smile in the mirror. "I suppose we're almost ready then?"

"Seems like it," Seth replied, his voice revealing a hint of nervousness despite his calm exterior. "Never been much for socials myself."

"Neither have I, really," she confessed, turning to face him. "But I think we'll manage just fine together."

"Guess we will," he agreed, pressing a kiss to her nose.

The churchyard buzzed with activity as they arrived, strings of lanterns casting a golden hue over the gathered townsfolk. Children darted between groups, laughter mingling with the soft strumming of a guitar somewhere in the background. The aroma of home-cooked food wafted through the air, tempting even the most reserved guest.

Brenda's eyes lit up at the sight of tables laden with treats, her stride purposeful as she made a beeline toward them. "Oh, look at those pies!" she exclaimed, her previous apprehension dissolving into excitement.

Seth couldn't help but chuckle at her enthusiasm. "Go on, I'll catch up," he said, his attention momentarily caught by a neighbor waving him over.

"All right, but save me a dance, cowboy," she called over her shoulder, her sass returning in full force as she joined the throng of friendly faces.

"Wouldn't miss it," he promised, watching her go. For a moment, he felt a swell of pride. Brenda was truly in her element, chatting animatedly with Mrs. Calloway about the intricacies of pie crusts.

As the evening unfolded around them, the church social became a tapestry of shared stories, community spirit, and the simple joys of rural life that bound them all together.

Seth stood by the refreshment table, a cup of punch in hand, watching as Brenda mingled with vigor among the townsfolk. He wasn't one for small talk, preferring the quiet companionship of his ranch to the bustling nature of social events. But as he observed the easy smiles and heard the genuine laughter around him, his lips began to tilt upwards.

"Never thought I'd see Seth Clinkinbeard at a church social," Kane Edwards said behind him. Kane was married to Brenda's sister, Faith.

"Neither did I," Seth admitted, the corner of his mouth quirking up further as he accepted the good-natured ribbing. "Brenda thought it would be good for us."

"Smart woman," Kane nodded approvingly. "You need a little fun mixed with all that hard work."

"Maybe you're right," Seth conceded.

The conversation flowed naturally from there, and before he knew it, Seth was trading stories with Kane and a few others, sharing anecdotes from the ranch that drew more than a few chuckles from the group. The initial hesitance melted away, replaced by a sense of kinship he hadn't realized he'd been missing.

As the night wore on, the music shifted to a lively tune, the fiddle's energetic cry beckoning the guests to the dance floor. Brenda caught his eye from across the yard. She sauntered over, her confidence as radiant as the stars above.

"Care to dance, Mr. Clinkinbeard?" she asked, extending her hand with a playful grin.

"Wouldn't miss it, Mrs. Clinkinbeard," he replied, setting down his punch and taking her hand in his.

They stepped onto the makeshift dance floor, joining other couples swaying to the rhythm of the music. Seth's hands found Brenda's waist as hers looped around his neck. They moved together in time with the fiddle, their movements hesitant at first but soon they were swaying as one.

Brenda's laughter rang out clear and bright when Seth spun her unexpectedly. He couldn't help but marvel at how natural it felt to hold her close, the warmth of her body against his stirring something deep within him.

"Look at you, light on your feet," she teased.

"Only when the partner's right," he quipped back, his heart pounding a rhythm akin to the music surrounding them. He thought of how he was going to hold her and make her cry out in pleasure when they got home that night. Dancing with Brenda was a joy that he needed to experience more often.

As the dance wound down, Seth and Brenda found themselves at the edge of the festivities, a rare quiet corner in the bustling church social. Brenda leaned against the wooden fence.

"I sure do like dancing with you," she said, a smile tugging at her lips.

Seth shrugged, his gaze meeting hers. "We'll have to do it more often. I was thinking that earlier. During our first dance."

Brenda chuckled. "I'll say. Sometimes you really surprise me, Seth."

"Same here," he admitted, running a hand through his hair, a sign of his unease. "You're not quite what I expected when they said 'bride from back East.'"

"Disappointed?"

"Quite the opposite." He let out a breath, his voice softer. "It's been...better than I thought it would be." Though, he'd really expected to have a wife who would stay in her place and never complain, and that was not what he'd gotten when he'd married Brenda.

"Me too." Her voice was sincere, her green eyes earnest. "This life, it's hard work, but I'm happy with you."

"I'm glad. Am I what you thought you'd have?"

She laughed softly. "No, I was thinking life would be more like a fairy tale. Being with you...It's not the dream I had as a girl, but it's a good one. A real one."

Seth nodded, feeling the truth in her words resonate within him. "It's a partnership. More than I ever thought to have."

"Just remember your partner at home when you get too wrapped up in work," she said, smiling up at him.

They stood in silence for a moment, the sounds of laughter and music floating over to them.

"Come on," Brenda finally said, pushing off the fence. "Let's head back. Those early mornings wait for no man...or woman."

Seth offered his arm, and she took it, her fingers squeezing gently in agreement.

The walk back to the ranch was filled with comfortable silence, the kind that spoke volumes about their growing bond. The stars above were brilliant.

When they got home, Seth drew Brenda into his arms, and kissed her passionately.

Brenda responded with equal fervor, her arms winding around his neck as they kissed. Seth's heart raced at the tenderness of her lips against his, the unspoken feelings that flowed between them in that moment. He broke away, breathless, and looked into Brenda's eyes.

"I never knew dancing could be so enjoyable," Seth admitted softly.

Brenda smiled, a warmth in her gaze that reached the depths of Seth's soul. "It was wonderful, wasn't it? I think we make a good team on the dance floor." She took his hand and pulled him toward the bedroom. "But it's a different kind of dance I'm ready for now," she said softly.

As they entered their bedroom, the air was thick with anticipation and an unspoken understanding. Seth watched Brenda's eyes, a mixture of desire and affection, as she turned to face him. Her hands reached for the buttons of his shirt, deftly undoing them one by one with practiced ease.

Seth's heart thudded in his chest. He mirrored her actions, slowly untying the ribbons that held her dress together, revealing the soft curves of her body beneath the fabric.

Their movements were unhurried, each touch deliberate and reverent. The flickering candlelight cast a warm glow over their entwined forms, creating shadows that danced across the walls in tandem with their growing passion.

When he held her after they made love, he whispered, "I never thought I'd marry a woman who would enjoy lovemaking as much as you do."

Brenda giggled. "Oh, I enjoy it!"

He kissed her forehead as he closed his eyes. "You're a good wife."

"I try…"

SETH WIPED THE SWEAT from his brow as he reached for a nail. A shadow fell across the fence, and he looked up to see Brenda approaching, a tin pail swinging in her hand.

"Thought you might be hungry," she said, setting the pail down with a gentle clank. She lifted the lid to reveal a pile of sandwiches, the bread still warm from the oven. She spread out a blanket.

"Chicken salad," she announced, "your favorite."

A simple meal, but it was the thought behind it that warmed Seth more than the Texas sun ever could. He couldn't remember the last time someone had made him something just because.

"Thank you, Brenda," he said. "Having a pretty wife like you bring a picnic to me sure does make the day go smoother."

She shrugged, a playful glint in her green eyes. "Figured it's about time I start pulling my weight around here," she teased.

Seth chuckled, biting into the sandwich. The flavors exploded in his mouth—tender chicken, crisp celery, a hint of dill—it was perfect. "I think you're doing more than your fair share," he replied, his mouth half full.

"Hey now, no talking with your mouth full," Brenda scolded with mock severity, wagging a finger at him.

"Sorry, ma'am," he said. They shared a laugh, the ease between them as comforting as the shade of the oak tree they sat under. At that moment, he thought marrying Brenda had been the smartest thing he'd ever done.

That evening, after supper, Brenda and Seth sat on the porch swing as they watched the sunset.

"Beautiful, isn't it?" Brenda asked, her gaze fixed on the pastel canvas above them.

"Sure is," he agreed, his tone matching hers in its quiet appreciation.

"I want to thank you for taking me to the church social on Friday. I know you didn't want to go. But it was fun."

"Sure was," he replied. "You've got a way of bringing joy into a room, Brenda. Can't say I didn't enjoy myself because of it."

Brenda's cheeks warmed at the compliment, and she looked away shyly. "I'm glad you had fun, Seth. I did too. More than I thought possible."

"Seems like we're doing all right," Seth said thoughtfully, his hand finding hers and giving it a gentle squeeze. "Building something together, making a life."

"More than all right," Brenda agreed, squeezing back.

"Never thought I'd be one for looking forward much," Seth confessed. "But with you, Brenda, I find myself thinking about tomorrow, and the day after, and...well, all the days to come."

"Me too, Seth. Me too."

They sat together in silence for a while, just enjoying each others company.

"Tomorrow's another big day," she said.

"Yep," Seth replied, his tone equally hushed. "Got to mend that fence by the lower field. And there's the new foal to tend to."

Brenda lifted her head to look at him, her green eyes reflecting the moonlight. "Sounds like we won't be running out of work anytime soon."

"Work keeps a man honest," he said with a small chuckle. "But it isn't all about work anymore."

"I'm glad." She said, thinking of the laughter and warmth they'd shared since the church social. "I think we should be going to more socials, making friends...maybe even starting a tradition or two of our own."

"Traditions, huh?" He seemed intrigued by the idea. "What kind of traditions?"

"Who knows? Maybe something simple, like a weekly picnic under the stars, or planting an orchard, watching it grow year after year." Her voice was laced with hope, painting pictures of a shared future in the quiet Texas night.

"An orchard..." Seth repeated softly, the word rolling off his tongue like a promise. "I like the sound of that."

They stood up together, bodies moving in sync as they headed back toward the house.

"Let's start with that picnic," Brenda suggested, her hand finding his in the darkness, fingers intertwining naturally. "This Saturday evening? After work?"

"Sounds perfect," he replied, his thumb tracing circles over her skin.

BRENDA HOISTED A BASKET of just-picked vegetables onto her hip. "Need help with that?" Brenda called out, her voice light and teasing.

Seth glanced up from where he was fighting with a weed, a grin cutting through the determination on his face. "Nope, this one's all mine," he said before giving the weed a victorious yank.

"Show-off," she chuckled, setting the basket down beside the porch.

"Only the best for you," he replied while making a face, which earned him a playful eye-roll.

The garden was thriving under their joint efforts, much like the easy camaraderie growing between them. They moved into the shade for a respite, fetching cool drinks from the well.

"I'm glad we decided to spend our Sunday afternoons together working on the garden," she said.

"It's something we both enjoy. It may be work, but it's work we do together with smiles. What else can a man ask for?"

Brenda planted a kiss on his lips. "Kisses."

He laughed. "I like your kisses..."

"You'd best not be liking any other girl's kisses!" she said in mock anger.

"I wouldn't dare. Only yours, Brenda."

Chapter Nine

Brenda busied herself with setting the table, the clink of cutlery against plates punctuating the quiet that hung in the air like the fine dust outside. Seth had just walked through the door.

"Evening, Brenda," he greeted.

"Evening, Seth," she replied without looking up.

They sat across from each other, a simple stew between them. The kitchen was warm, the heat from the stove fighting the coolness that began to settle with the encroaching night.

"Stew's good," Seth said, spooning a hearty portion into his mouth.

"Thanks," Brenda responded, her lips curving into a half-smile. "So, how was your day?"

"Hot. The cattle are restless with this weather." He paused, wiping sweat from his brow even now. "And yours?"

"Same as always—hot. It's already October. When is it going to cool off?"

"By the end of the month, it should be tolerable." he said, chuckling. "Do you not like the weather here?"

Brenda sighed. "It's just so hot all the time."

As they finished, Seth pushed his chair back and reached into his pocket, producing two slips of paper. He slid them across the table toward Brenda. She eyed them curiously before picking them up, her eyes scanning the print.

"Tickets?" she asked, surprised.

"Play in Fort Worth. It's called Lost, Strayed or Stolen. I know you said you'd never really done anything like that, but I thought maybe we could try it together. We could use a night out, you know, enjoy something different."

"Really?" A genuine smile tugged at her lips, her earlier reluctance forgotten. "That's...actually really nice. Thank you, Seth."

"Figured it was about time I showed you some proper courting," he said, the corners of his eyes crinkling with amusement.

"Courting, huh?" Brenda teased, the sassiness she was known for making a quick appearance. "I might just hold you to that."

"Good," Seth replied earnestly, his gaze meeting hers. "Because I think there's more to our marriage than just eating supper every night."

"I'm so excited! I wanted to see a play in Boston once, and I saved up all my money...and I forgot to save for the train fare, so I never got to go. I would have eventually, I'm sure, but I wouldn't have even been able to afford a dress to wear."

"Do you think you need a new dress for this?" he asked.

"I know I do! But that's all right. Cassandra will make it for me."

"Will she mind?" he asked.

"Cassandra? She loves to sew. She's been talking about being a modiste since we were children, and I know it will happen. Eventually."

He frowned for a moment. "We'll pay her for the dress if she doesn't charge too much." He knew he didn't need to be tight with money, but frugality had always felt right to him.

"It would make her so happy!"

"Then it's settled. We'll go to the play, and you'll have a new dress for it." Seth's voice held a note of promise.

Brenda clapped, excited for the opportunity to see a play.

BRENDA STOOD BEFORE the mirror, her fingers working deftly to coax her blond hair into loose curls that framed her face. The dress Cassandra had made was simple, its fabric catching the light in a way that made it seem more elegant than its plain cut would suggest. It was a far cry from the garments she had known in the orphanage.

"Never thought I'd be wearing something like this to a play," she mused aloud, the sound of her voice grounding her in the small room filled with anticipation.

"Nor did I ever picture myself taking a woman as striking as you to one," Seth's voice came from the doorway.

Brenda turned, her green eyes meeting his. "Don't you go starting with sweet talk now, Seth," she teased, though the blush that crept up her cheeks betrayed her pleasure at the compliment.

"Only speaking the truth," he replied, holding out his arm for her to take.

Together, they headed out to the wagon he'd already hitched up. For a moment she wished they had a fancy buggy, but it didn't really matter to her too much. She was excited to be going.

The town was alive with the buzz of folks going about their business, but Brenda barely noticed them—her focus was on the building ahead, adorned with posters and lights that seemed to beckon them closer.

As they entered the theater, the grandeur of the place struck Brenda silent. Velvet-covered seats filled the space, and an ornate stage loomed before them, draped with heavy curtains waiting to reveal secrets within. They found their seats among the throng of well-dressed attendees, and for a moment, Brenda felt a world away from the life she had always known.

"Never seen anything quite like this," she whispered, leaning toward Seth so only he could hear.

"Me neither," he admitted. "But I reckon it's gonna be a night to remember."

Brenda's heart swelled as she looked around, taking in every detail—the way the chandelier overhead scattered light across the room, the sound of the orchestra tuning their instruments, the soft murmur of conversation around them. This was a moment of pure enchantment, a slice of life she had never imagined being part of.

"Thank you for bringing me here," she said softly. "I feel out of place, but I'm so happy to be here I can't even express it."

"Thank you for coming with me," Seth responded, his smile reflecting the warmth in his eyes.

And as the house lights dimmed, signaling the beginning of the performance, Brenda felt a hand gently find hers. She didn't pull away. Instead, she allowed her fingers to intertwine with Seth's, acknowledging the connection that grew stronger with each shared experience. Tonight, enveloped in the magic of the theater, Brenda realized that perhaps there was a place for her in this new, wondrous world after all.

THE FINAL APPLAUSE echoed in Brenda's ears as she and Seth stepped out of the theater, her hand still nestled comfortably in his. The night air was cool, and it felt so good after the long, hot summer.

"Did you enjoy it?" Seth asked, a twinkle in his eye.

"More than I ever thought I would," Brenda confessed, her heart still racing from the crescendo of the final act. "I always knew it was something I wanted to do, but I didn't expect it to be quite so wonderful!"

"Let's not end the night just yet," Seth suggested. "How about we grab a bite before we head back? There's a place not far from here that does a good steak."

"Sounds perfect," she said with a smile, the idea of prolonging the evening with him appealing to her more than she expected.

They walked to where his wagon awaited, the horses calm and patient. Seth helped her up before climbing aboard himself. With a gentle flick of the reins, they were off.

"Never figured I'd find myself at a play in Fort Worth," Brenda mused aloud as the wagon rolled through the streets.

"Life's full of surprises," Seth replied, glancing over at her with an easy grin.

"Reckon it is," she agreed. "When you're not busy surprising me with plays and dinners, what do you dream about, Seth?"

"Me?" Seth chuckled, the sound rich and comforting. "I dream of making the ranch into something my pa would've been proud of. And lately," he paused, "lately, I've been dreaming of days like this. With you."

Brenda felt warmth spread through her chest, a soft blush blooming on her cheeks. "You're quite the charmer, aren't you?"

"Only speaking truth, Brenda. What about you? What dreams keep you company?"

She gazed out at the darkening horizon, contemplating. "A place to call my own," she said. "A family, maybe. Not blood, necessarily. But folks who care whether you come home at night."

"Like a community," Seth said, nodding.

"Exactly," Brenda agreed. "And laughter. Lots of it. Life's too short for anything less. And children. I don't want a dozen like Amy does, but three or four would make me very happy."

"Thank you for tonight, Seth," Brenda said as they approached the restaurant, its windows glowing warmly.

"Thank you for saying yes," he replied, helping her down from the wagon with a tender touch that lingered.

"COZY?" SETH ASKED, a half-smirk playing on his lips.

"Very," she replied, the corners of her mouth tilting upward. "You're not too bad as a pillow."

"Tomorrow's Saturday," Seth said after a pause. "Thought I might take a day away from the ranch work."

"Really?" Brenda lifted her head to look at him. "You know if you take a day off work, you have to actually not work, right?" It was hard to think of Seth taking a day off, but it sounded wonderful to her.

"Yep," he confirmed, grinning. "Figured we could explore a bit. See the land beyond the pastures."

"Sounds...nice." It was more than nice. It was unexpected and thrilling, but she tucked that thought away, her sassiness simmering down to a gentle smile.

"That's the plan then."

BRENDA WATCHED FROM the porch as Seth led two horses toward her, their hooves kicking up small clouds of dust.

"Ready for our day off?" he called out, extending his hand to help her mount.

"Born ready," Brenda said, accepting his assistance with a playful swat at his arm.

They rode side by side. "Look at that view," Brenda said, reining her horse to a stop atop a hill. "It would be so much more beautiful in the spring when everything is green, but even with the world all brown, it's beautiful!"

"Beats looking at cattle all day," Seth agreed, his gaze not on the horizon but on her profile.

"Doesn't everything?" she teased, meeting his eyes with a glint of mischief.

"Almost," he said.

Together, they descended the hill. Their horses seemed to catch onto their light-heartedness, tails swishing merrily as they trotted across the open fields.

"Ever think about what it'd be like to just ride off, see where the land takes you?" Brenda asked.

"Sometimes," Seth admitted. "But I think I've found something worth staying put for."

Brenda didn't need to ask what—or who—that something was. She already knew, felt it in the way her heart skipped when he smiled, how the future seemed brighter with him in it.

"Me too, Seth. Me too."

Brenda smiled as she saw the river, and she and Seth dismounted by the water's edge. Their horses grazed nearby, content in the lush grass.

"Feels like the world's just ours for the taking," Brenda said, easing down onto the soft earth. She stretched her legs out. "I'm so glad you decided to take the day off. Have you ever done this before? Not when you were sick, of course, but just because you wanted to?"

Seth shrugged. "Not really. My pa only cared about the land. Ma died when my sister was born, and Pa cared about the legacy he was leaving me and nothing else." He shook his head. "I think that's where I got it from."

"How old were you when she died?"

"Two. I don't remember anything about her. We had a housekeeper until my sister married and Pa died. Then there didn't seem to be any point."

"I'm sorry you've been alone."

He sighed. "I had my work to keep me company."

"I'm not sure that was the best thing for you!" Brenda said. "Does it feel good to not be alone anymore?"

"Sure does," Seth replied, sitting beside her with a relaxed slant to his shoulders. He pulled off his hat, running a hand through his hair before settling back, his gaze fixed on the water. "You ever been to a spot like this before?"

"Never quite like this," she confessed with a smile. The simplicity of the scene, the gentle flow of the river, it was all new to her. But it felt comfortable there with him.

They shared tales of their childhoods—his on the expansive ranch, hers in the crowded orphanage.

"Did you really trade your sister's pie for a frog?" Seth asked, one eyebrow cocked in amused disbelief.

"Guilty," Brenda admitted. "But in my defense, it was a very convincing magic frog."

"Ah, I see. And did it grant wishes?"

"Only the wish of seeing my sister's face turn the color of her cherry filling," she chuckled. "I thought Amy was going to strangle me in my sleep, and let's be honest. I deserved it."

Seth shook his head, still grinning. Without a word, he stood up and wandered a few steps away, stooping down to where the wildflowers grew thick and abundant along the riverbank.

"Here," Seth said upon returning, holding out a small bouquet of wildflowers. The colors were vibrant—a mix of blues, yellows, and purples, woven together by his rough hands into a token both delicate and strong.

Brenda looked up at him, surprise etched on her features before shifting into a warm, appreciative smile. "For me?" Her voice was soft, touched by the simple kindness of the gesture.

"Thought they'd look nicer with you than with the dirt," Seth replied.

"Thank you, Seth," she said, taking the flowers and brushing her fingers over the petals. "They're beautiful."

"Figured they matched your spirit," he added, watching her reaction closely.

"Is that so?" Brenda asked. "Wild and untamed?"

"Exactly," he said, settling back down next to her with a contented sigh.

"SURE IS A BEAUTIFUL evening," Seth remarked.

"Sure is," Brenda said, her lips curving into a smile. She was almost disappointed to walk inside, but she was hungry, and she knew he must be as well."Go on and wash up, I'll call you when supper's ready." she instructed.

"Need any help?" Seth offered.

"I think I can manage," Brenda replied, her tone playful yet firm. "But thank you, Seth."

She watched him nod and retreat to clean up, then turned her attention to the task at hand. Her hands moved deftly, more confident than she would admit, as she prepared a dish she remembered from her time at the mansion in Beckham—baked chicken with herbs and a side of roasted vegetables.

Brenda glanced out the window. Her heart felt light, almost giddy, with the knowledge that this was her life now. She wasn't just the orphan girl from Massachusetts. She was a woman who found joy in the company of a man who valued her more than she'd ever expected.

"Supper's ready," she called out, setting the table.

Seth entered the room, clean and looking refreshed, his hair still damp at the edges. He took a seat, eyeing the food with approval. "Smells wonderful, Brenda."

"Hope it tastes as good as it smells," she said, serving him a generous portion.

Brenda watched Seth trace the tines of his fork through the herbs sprinkled atop the chicken. His eyes lifted, met hers, and he chuckled.

"Never thought I'd be so grateful for a meal that didn't come from a can."

They ate, each bite savored, each moment stretching out comfortably between them. The roasted vegetables were tender, the chicken seasoned just right, and the silence was filled with the kind of warmth that only shared satisfaction could bring. Their bond, once tentative and unsure, now felt as natural as the sun setting beyond the window.

"Thank you, Brenda. For this." Seth gestured to the plates, the table, and the cozy room around them.

"Wasn't anything," she said.

"Means everything to me," he said softly, reaching across the table to squeeze her hand. She squeezed back.

Later, as night draped itself over the ranch, they found themselves entwined beneath the sheets, moonlight spilling across the bed. Seth's touch was gentle, his gaze steady—full of something that Brenda had dared not name until now.

After, as Seth lay beside her, breaths deep and even, Brenda lay awake. Her mind wandered, tracing the path of their short marriage, the laughter, and the growing closeness. Yet, there was a small, niggling worry at the back of her mind. Four months had passed, and she had no signs of expecting.

She should have been with child by now, shouldn't she? Brenda turned to look at Seth, his features softened by sleep. A crease formed between her brows, but she smoothed it away with a sigh. No, she wouldn't burden him with her worries—not yet.

"Tomorrow," she whispered to herself. "I'll think about it tomorrow."

Chapter Ten

Brenda finished rinsing the last of the breakfast dishes. She wiped her hands on her apron, and glanced out the window to where the Texas sun was climbing higher in the sky. With a determined breath, she removed her apron, folded it neatly, and set out for Amy's house.

"Knock, knock," Brenda called out, tapping lightly on the wooden doorframe. Before she could contemplate on the words bubbling just beneath her tongue, the door swung open.

"Oh, Brenda!" Amy's voice was like a fresh breeze as she stood in the doorway, her cheeks flushed with excitement. "You won't believe it—I'm pregnant!"

Brenda's heart leaped for her friend, and all thoughts of her worries momentarily evaporated. "That's wonderful news, Amy!" she said, stepping into the house and enveloping her friend in a warm hug. The scent of freshly baked bread lingered in the air, a testament to Amy's knack for baking.

"Can you believe it? We're going to have a little one by summer!" Amy's eyes sparkled with tears of joy.

"Summer babies are the best," Brenda said, pulling back to look at Amy, her own smile wide. "All those new beginnings."

"Exactly." Amy patted her still-flat belly with a tender hand. "I just had to tell someone, and I knew you'd be happy for us."

"Of course, I am," Brenda affirmed, feeling a mix of delight for Amy and a twinge of longing. But this wasn't the moment for her worries—today was about Amy's joy. "You're going to make the most amazing mother."

"Thank you, Brenda." Amy's face softened, her gratitude genuine. "I've always wanted a family of my own, you know? Not that I don't consider the four I have now my own, but this one I'll give birth to and know from infancy."

"Who wouldn't?" Brenda replied, knowing full well the depth of that desire. "And I reckon you'll have the liveliest house in the county before long."

"Let's hope so," laughed Amy, leading Brenda toward the kitchen. "Now, enough about me—what brings you here today?"

"Just felt like a visit," Brenda said. "And maybe to snag a taste of whatever's in that oven." Her gaze flitted to the stove, where a golden crust peeked out from the oven door, and she winked at Amy.

"Always welcome," Amy chuckled, slicing into the warm bread. "Especially when there's good news to share."

"Couldn't agree more," Brenda murmured, letting the comfort of companionship soothe her—if only for a little while.

BRENDA'S FEET KICKED up small clouds of dust as she made her way to Cassandra's home. The summer heat wrapped around her like a heavy shawl, but it was the weight in her heart that truly slowed her steps. She pushed open the gate and stepped into the modest garden, where blooms fought valiantly against the relentless Texas sun.

"Morning, Cassie," Brenda called out as she entered the cool shade of the parlor. Cassandra looked up from her sewing, a fine needlework of delicate flowers taking shape under her deft fingers.

"Hey there, Brenda," Cassandra greeted. "What's on your mind?"

It spilled out of Brenda then, the words tumbling over each other like pebbles in a rush of water. "I'm just...I'm worried, you know? About not having a baby yet." Her green eyes searched Cassandra's face for something—anything—that might ease this ache.

Cassandra set her sewing aside, her gaze steady and kind. "You're doing all you can, Brenda. These things sometimes take time."

But the platitudes were like cotton—soft and without substance. Brenda nodded, though her insides churned with impatience. "Yeah, I suppose."

"Come here," Cassandra said, patting the seat beside her. Side by side, they sat in silence.

"Thanks, Cassie." Brenda forced a smile, her gratitude real even if the comfort wasn't.

"Anytime," Cassandra replied, picking up her sewing again.

Leaving Cassandra's home, Brenda wandered toward Deborah's place, following the well-worn path between their houses like a lifeline. She found Deborah sitting on the porch, the click-clack of her knitting needles punctuating the afternoon stillness.

"Deb," Brenda said, her voice hitching slightly, "do you ever wonder if some things just aren't meant to be?"

Deborah looked up from her work, her brown eyes gentle behind the spectacles perched on her nose. "Sometimes," she admitted, "but why do you ask?"

"Ah, it's silly," Brenda waved a hand dismissively. "Just thinking about babies and all."

"Give it time, Brenda," Deborah offered softly, her hands never stopping their dance with the wool. "Your home will be filled with little ones before you know it."

"Sure," Brenda sighed, the word hollow as a drum. She watched a sparrow flit from branch to branch in the oak tree nearby.

"Are you all right?" Deborah asked, concern lacing her words.

"Of course," Brenda lied with a brightness she didn't feel. "Just got to keep busy, right?"

"Right," Deborah agreed, though her doubtful look said she heard the unspoken words hidden beneath Brenda's cheer.

"Thanks, Deb," Brenda said as she stood. "You keep those needles flying."

"Always do," Deborah replied with a small smile.

Back on the dusty road, Brenda's thoughts swirled like leaves in a gust of wind. Neither conversation had brought clarity, but perhaps action would. She squared her shoulders and headed home.

Brenda rolled up the sleeves of her worn dress and set to work. Her hands gripped the broom with a familiarity that required no thought, allowing her mind to wander amidst the rhythmic strokes that sent motes of dust dancing in the late afternoon sunlight.

"Out, out, every speck," she muttered to herself. It wasn't just the floors that felt the brunt of Brenda's restless energy. Beds were heaved aside, their undersides scrutinized and scrubbed until they could harbor no more secrets. Walls, too, were attended to with a fervor that had them gleaming under her care.

By the time Seth returned, the house was transformed, its normally cozy disarray replaced by an almost sterile cleanliness. He hung his hat on the peg by the door, a distracted hum escaping him as he scanned the spotless room.

"Did a cyclone blow through here or is it just you?" Seth teased.

"Ha," Brenda retorted with feigned lightness, "just thought the place could use a good fall cleaning, is all."

"Smells like lemon and elbow grease," he observed.

"What exactly does elbow grease smell like?" Brenda asked.

"Like our house without the lemon," he replied, winking at her.

They sat down to a supper of hearty stew, the kind that usually warmed the room with laughter and banter. Seth ladled the stew into his bowl, his movements mechanical, his thoughts far from the food.

"Everything all right with the herd?" Brenda asked, hoping to draw him back from whatever distant plains his mind roamed.

"Ah, yes, fine," he responded without meeting her eye. "Just...thinking on some things."

"Anything I can help with?" Her question was genuine.

"Nothing to fuss over." Seth's reply came quick, a barrier going up as if to hold back any intruders to his private concerns.

Brenda nodded. She wanted to tell him about her day, about the gnawing void that spurred her cleaning frenzy, but the words lodged in her throat, unsaid. Instead, she watched him, noting the crease in his brow and the way he pushed his food around the bowl.

"Sure," she said finally, the single word heavy with unvoiced thoughts. She stood to clear the table, her motions precise and controlled, the clatter of dishes filling the space where conversation once lived.

After the dishes were done, Brenda swept the broom across the wooden floor with vigor, her mind a whirlwind as chaotic as the dust she stirred up. Her blond hair had come loose from its bun, strands sticking to her damp forehead. She moved furniture, the usual spark in her green gaze dulled by an inner turmoil.

"Brenda, you've been at this all evening," Seth's voice broke through the rhythmic swish of the broom. "Isn't it time to rest now?"

She paused, leaning on the broom handle, her back to him. "Just need to get it done, is all," Brenda replied. The truth clawed at her insides, begging for release, yet she couldn't bring herself to voice it. Not yet.

Seth watched her for a moment longer before nodding and stepping back, his unease a silent shadow in the dimly lit room.

Later, as they lay side by side in the darkness, the silence was a tangible presence between them. When Seth's hand reached out, seeking hers, Brenda turned away, her heart heavy. For the first time since they'd shared a bed, she couldn't bear the intimacy, not with the weight of her secret pressing down on her. She must be barren. There was no other reason for her not to be expecting.

"I just...I need to think," she whispered into the pillow, hoping he would understand her need for space. Her thoughts raced, grasping for solutions where none seemed to exist.

A memory surfaced, clear and promising – the book of receipts at the general store, its pages filled with wisdom on the medicinal properties of herbs. Her knowledge in that area was strong. Maybe there was an answer waiting for her within those pages. Yes, she decided, tomorrow she would buy that book. It was a plan, something to hold onto amidst the uncertainty.

"All right," came Seth's soft reply, confusion and concern mingling in his voice.

THE TEXAS SUN CLIMBED high as Brenda made her way to the general store. The wooden door creaked open, announcing her arrival. She beelined for the shelf where the book of receipts nestled between jars of molasses and tins of tea.

"Morning, Brenda," greeted Mr. Parsons from behind the counter, tipping his hat.

"Morning," she replied with a polite nod.

Her fingers danced over the leather-bound spine before she plucked the tome from its perch. Flipping through the pages, Brenda found what she was looking for: an herbal remedy for barrenness, a concoction of promise. The ingredients were listed with care, but one, in particular, caught her eye – an herb she didn't recognize.

"Never seen this one before," she murmured to herself, tracing the name with her finger.

She purchased the book without hesitation, the coins clinking softly as they exchanged hands. Outside, Brenda shielded her eyes and thought of Susan Dailey. If anyone knew about healing herbs, it would be Elizabeth's sister, blessed with a brood of her own.

A short stroll down the dusty road brought her to Susan's homestead. Susan was seated on the porch, peeling apples with practiced ease.

"Hey there, Susan," Brenda called out, as she approached.

"Hello, Brenda! What brings you?" Susan asked, setting aside her work.

"Got a minute?" Brenda asked, her tone casual but her green eyes serious.

"Of course," Susan smiled warmly, patting the seat beside her.

Brenda took the offered spot, the wood of the porch warm beneath her. "I'm looking for an herb," she began, hesitating only slightly. "One that might help...with womanly troubles."

Susan's brow furrowed with concern, but she nodded encouragingly.

"Know anyone in these parts who deals with healing herbs?" Brenda asked, hoping her friend could point her in the right direction.

"Let me think..." Susan tapped her chin thoughtfully. "Most folks go to Old Man Jenkins for poultices. But for something special, there's a lady down the road. Got a knack for herbs, they say. She delivered all my babies."

"Would you happen to know where I can find her?" Brenda leaned in, a spark of hope igniting within her.

"Sure do," Susan replied, her voice dropping to a conspiratorial whisper. "I'll write down directions. You be careful now, you hear?"

"Always am," Brenda answered with a grin.

"You sure you're all right?" Susan asked softly.

"Thank you, Susan. Really," Brenda said, her gratitude sincere.

"Anytime, Brenda," Susan replied, her eyes kind. "You just let me know if you need anything else."

With newfound purpose, Brenda tucked the precious information into the pocket of her apron. She waved goodbye to Susan and set off back down the road, her mind already racing with possibilities.

Brenda's heart skipped a beat as she approached the modest homestead nestled at the edge of a sprawling Texas meadow. She was happy fall was finally on them, but it was still hotter than she would like. Squinting against the bright light, she rapped gently on the wooden door, its paint weathered from years under the relentless sun.

"Who is it?" called a voice from inside.

"Brenda Clinkinbeard," she answered. "I'm looking for Hortense Blakely."

The door creaked open, and there stood a woman with hands that told stories of life brought into this world. Her eyes were kind, her smile gentle, and her hair streaked with silver strands of wisdom.

"Come in," Hortense beckoned, stepping aside to allow Brenda entry. "What brings you out this way?"

"Got a bit of a personal matter," Brenda said, her confidence faltering just a tad as she crossed the threshold. The room was cool with jars of herbs lining shelves along the wall.

"Sit, sit." Hortense pointed to a chair by a large wooden table. "Tell me what's ailin' ya, and we'll see if Mother Nature has an answer."

Brenda hesitated, then decided to trust in the confidentiality of the midwife's profession. "Well, it's just that...I've been trying to conceive, and nothing's come of it yet."

"Ah." The midwife's face softened even further. "Let's see what we can do about that."

She moved with purpose, her hands selecting jars and pouches. Brenda watched, captivated by the smooth efficiency of her movements.

"Here's red clover, full of isoflavones, good for fertility," Hortense explained, handing her a small bundle. "And raspberry leaf, to strengthen the womb." Another pouch joined the first.

"Make these into a tea, morning and night," Hortense instructed, her tone both commanding and comforting.

"Thank you," Brenda breathed, relief washing over her. "How much do I owe you?"

"Nothing for now," Hortense replied with a wave of her hand. "You bring me good news of a babe, and we'll call it even."

Brenda smiled, her spirit lifted. She felt lighter as she left the midwife's home, the pouches of hope in her pocket.

Chapter Eleven

Brenda's fingers wrapped around the warm ceramic of her teacup, steam curling up like a lazy cat stretching in the sun. She brought the cup to her lips, the herbal aroma mingling with the scent of home-baked bread that filled the kitchen. The tea was a new habit, one she'd taken to morning and night with a kind of religious fervor.

"Another batch of that special tea, huh?" Seth leaned against the doorframe, his eyes flitting between the cup and her face. A teasing smile played on his lips, but there was a hint of curiosity behind his casual stance.

"Can't seem to get enough of it," Brenda replied, keeping her voice light. "Just love the taste."

Seth raised an eyebrow but didn't press further, turning his attention back to the ranch work that awaited him outside. Brenda watched him go, relieved. If he knew the true purpose of her tea drinking—that it was a fertility blend—she wasn't sure how he'd react. Not yet, anyway. Would he even want her to remain his wife if she couldn't have the children he wanted?

Later, as the Texas heat waned into a gentler warmth, Brenda found herself at Hannah's modest home. She knocked lightly.

Hannah greeted her sister with a smile, the lacework in her hands momentarily forgotten. "What brings you by, Brenda?"

"Thought we might stir up some Christmas cheer. How about throwing a party for the church this year?" Brenda asked, already picturing the festivities, the joy it could bring.

"Sounds lovely," Hannah said, though her gaze drifted, hinting at thoughts that wandered far from holiday merriment. "But you'll have to spearhead it. And Brenda..."

"Yes?"

"I'm still wrestling with my faith. You know that." Hannah's words were soft, spoken more to the floor than to Brenda. "I married a good man in Amos, but God and I...we're not on speaking terms."

"Doesn't mean we can't spread a little goodwill, right?" Brenda nudged her sister's knee with a playful smile. "We'll make it a party that even God would attend if He got an invite."

Hannah chuckled, her tension easing. "All right, let's plan a Christmas party."

"Good." Brenda's heart swelled with a sense of purpose, her mind already racing with ideas. This party would stop her from spending all her time worrying about not having a baby.

BRENDA, WITH HER BLOND hair tied back and a notepad in hand, could barely contain her excitement as she bounded from one sister to the next. Her green eyes sparkled with the light of the upcoming festivities, and her voice carried the tune of holiday spirit through the warm air of Fort Worth.

"All right, Amy, you're on pies. And Jane, I want your cornbread dressing," Brenda directed, scribbling down notes as she went, assigning culinary tasks with the confidence of a general leading her troops.

"Are you sure we can pull this off in a month, Brenda?" Jane asked skeptically, wiping her hands on her apron.

"Of course, we can!" Brenda replied with a chuckle. "We've got hands enough, and hearts big enough to feed the whole county!"

Laughter and chatter filled the room as the women gathered around her, each accepting their part in the grand plan.

"Wait until you hear about the main course, ladies," Brenda said with an impish grin, her eyes darting toward the doorway where Seth stood, leaning against the frame with his arms crossed, a half-smile on his face.

"Speaking of which," Brenda approached Seth, her gait confident and purposeful. "Seth, how would you feel about donating one of your steers for the Christmas feast?"

Seth raised an eyebrow, amusement dancing in his eyes. "You planning to butcher it yourself, Brenda?"

"Ha! I might not enjoy cooking, but I know my way around a kitchen well enough to ensure that steer is the star of the show," she retorted with a playful jab to his arm.

"All right, all right," he said, shaking his head. "I reckon it's for a good cause. Consider one of my finest steers yours."

"Thank you, Seth! You're a saint among cowboys," Brenda teased, her sassiness wrapped in genuine gratitude.

"Saint, huh?" Seth chuckled. "Don't let that get around, or I'll never live it down."

As Seth strolled away, Brenda turned back to her list, her heart swelled with pride.

"All right, everyone, let's make this a Christmas to remember!" Brenda declared, rallying the women with a determined nod. The room erupted in cheers, everyone ready to bring their best to the table—literally.

And so, with lists in hand and a clear vision in her heart, Brenda set forth to create a celebration that would embody the love and companionship she'd felt since arriving in Texas.

Brenda's fingers danced over the delicate paper ornaments, a soft hum escaping her lips. Seth leaned against the door frame, watching her whirl about the room, a flurry of festive energy.

"Everything all right, Brenda?" His voice was tinged with a mix of concern and curiosity as he took in the scene before him: garlands strung across the walls, an evergreen tree filled with homemade baubles, and tables groaning under the weight of her meticulous plans.

"Never better!" she said, not pausing in her labors. "Just got to make sure we've got enough sugar for the cookies, and yarn for the garlands, and...oh, can't forget the secret gift exchange!" Her list seemed endless, but her eyes sparkled with the thrill of it all. It felt good not to worry about having a baby so much.

"Seems like a lot for one person," Seth said, his gaze following her every move.

"Maybe," Brenda conceded with a grin, "but when has that ever stopped me? Besides, I've got the whole church pitching in!"

"True enough," he said with a chuckle. "Just don't wear yourself out before the party even starts."

"I'll do my best," she responded.

Later, Brenda found Hannah in the quiet of her home, crochet hook in hand, calm as ever. As Brenda laid out her grand plans, Hannah's brows rose, her hands stilling mid-stitch at the extent of her sister's ambition.

"Goodness, Brenda, that's quite the undertaking," Hannah said, a touch of awe threading through her words.

"It's our first Christmas as married women," Brenda replied with a laugh. "I want this Christmas to sparkle, especially for the little ones."

"Nobody but you could pull this off," Hannah said with a fond smile, her admiration clear despite her shock.

"Help me with the lace for the tree, and we'll call it even," Brenda suggested.

"Sounds good to me," Hannah agreed, already envisioning the intricate patterns she'd create.

"Perfect! This will be a Christmas like no other," Brenda declared, her heart swelled with love for her community and the shared joy the season would bring.

BRENDA KNOCKED ON THE doorframe of Susan's bustling kitchen, a smile playing on her lips. "You'll never guess who I've roped into the Christmas baking brigade," she announced with a hint of mischief in her eyes.

Susan looked up from where she was sorting through a pile of flour sacks and grinned back. "Who'd you manage to convince this time?" she asked, wiping her hands on her apron.

"Jane," Brenda said, gesturing over her shoulder where Jane stood hesitantly, a flour-dusted rolling pin in hand. "She's decided to take charge of the cookies."

"Is that so?" Susan raised an eyebrow in playful skepticism, turning her attention to Jane. "Isn't she doing the dressing as well?"

"I might not know my way around a kitchen as well as some," Jane confessed, "but I can learn. And everyone loves cookies, right?"

"Right you are, dear," Susan agreed, her voice warm. She moved toward Jane and took the rolling pin, guiding her hands with an experienced touch. "We'll make a baker out of you yet."

"Thanks, Susan," Jane replied, her tentative smile growing more confident. "I'm sure glad to be helping out. It's been months since I got to Texas, but things like this...they make it feel more like home."

"Christmas has a way of doing that," Brenda chimed in, leaning against the counter and watching the two work together. "And who knows, maybe all this cookie baking will help you make up your mind about those suitors of yours."

"Maybe," Jane said, glancing out the window. "Or maybe I'll just become Fort Worth's most eligible cookie baker instead."

The three women shared a laugh. In this simple act of baking, they found the thread that wove them closer, binding them together in the fabric of their small community.

BRENDA SAT BACK ON her heels, surveying the room bustling with preparations for the upcoming Christmas party. Her gaze landed on Susan, who was orchestrating a merry chaos of children and decorations with a grace that made Brenda grin. The woman was a whirlwind of efficiency, her skirts swishing as she moved from one task to another, her laughter mingling with the cacophony of festive sounds.

"Got your name for the gift exchange," Brenda called out over the noise, catching Susan's attention.

"Did you now?" Susan wiped her hands on her apron, leaving a streak of flour across the faded fabric. "Well, don't go fussing over me."

"Wouldn't dream of it," Brenda quipped, though her mind churned with the problem at hand. What do you give a woman like Susan, who seemed to already have a full life?

Hours later, Brenda found herself alone in her room, the question still nagging at her. She rifled through her trunk, hoping inspiration would strike among her modest belongings. There wasn't much. Then an idea sparked as she pulled out a length of sturdy cotton she'd been saving for...something. She didn't quite know what, until now.

"An apron," she murmured to herself, holding the fabric up to the lamplight. No woman ever had enough aprons!

THE NEXT MORNING, BRENDA set to work with needle and thread, her fingers moving deftly despite her usual aversion to sewing. She cut the pattern carefully, ensuring the apron would be generous enough to cover the front of Susan's dresses completely. As she sewed, her thoughts wandered to the warmth of the community, how each person brought something special to the table—just as Susan brought her care and compassion.

"Making a tent there, Brenda?" Seth's voice interrupted her thoughts, his teasing tone drawing a reluctant smile from her.

"Hardly," Brenda retorted without looking up. "Just a little something for Susan. I got her name in the drawing." Brenda had arranged the drawing for the women, and had done a separate one for the men.

"Ah, practical and thoughtful," Seth observed, leaning against the doorframe. "Sounds like someone else I know."

"Watch it, cowboy," Brenda warned with mock severity, tying off a knot and snipping the thread. "I might just make you one next."

"Promise?" Seth asked.

"Maybe," Brenda said, allowing herself a small chuckle. But her focus was on the apron now taking shape, a simple but meaningful token of appreciation for a woman who gave so much of herself. It was the least Brenda could do—her way of weaving love into the fabric of their shared lives.

BRENDA TOOK THE FIRST sip of her tea, a concoction more of hope than flavor. She didn't know if it was working, but she certainly hoped it was.

"Tea again?" Seth's voice carried from behind her as he entered the kitchen.

"Can't start my day without it," Brenda replied, her tone light, masking the true reason behind her new routine.

"Must be some kind of magic brew." Seth chuckled.

"Could be," she teased back, taking another sip before setting the cup down. "Now, if only it could sew."

"Need a hand there?" He nodded toward the apron spread across the table, half-made.

"Unless you've got hidden talents, I think I'll manage." Brenda picked up the needle and thread, resuming her work on the apron. Her fingers moved purposefully, stitching the fabric with care.

"Never pegged you for the sewing type," Seth observed, his eyes following her movements.

"Neither did I," Brenda admitted with a small smile. "But Susan needs something practical, and we made the rule the gifts have to be hand-made."

"Sounds like you're putting your heart into it," Seth said, leaning forward to examine the apron closer.

"Maybe a little," Brenda said. The soft cotton felt good under her touch, and she found comfort in the repetitive motion of the needle piercing through the material. "It's for Christmas, after all."

"Christmas does have a way of bringing out the best in folks," Seth said, his gaze lingering on her face for a moment before he stood. "Well, I'll leave you to it."

With Seth gone, she turned her attention back to the apron, the morning quiet except for the sound of her sewing. This simple act of creating something with her own hands felt surprisingly fulfilling.

Chapter Twelve

Today was the day of the Christmas party, an event that had occupied all Brenda's waking thoughts for weeks. Yet, instead of the usual buzz of excitement, a different sensation churned in her stomach—a mix of nerves and nausea that had been plaguing her for days.

"Wait, this isn't just nerves," she muttered to herself, pressing a hand to her abdomen. Could she be expecting?

She quickly donned a simple dress, its fabric worn but clean, and made her way to see Hortense the midwife. The walk was short, but Brenda felt each step with a heightened sense of awareness. She rapped on the door lightly, her heart thumping louder than her knuckles against the wood.

"Come in, Brenda," Hortense called from within.

"Morning, Hortense," Brenda greeted, her voice betraying none of the turmoil inside her.

"Good morning, dear. You look a bit peaked. What brings you around so early?" Hortense peered at her over a pair of wire-rimmed spectacles.

"I need some advice...maybe more." Brenda hesitated, then blurted out, "I think I might be with child."

Hortense's eyes softened, and she took Brenda's hands in her own. "So you think the tea did the trick. Well, let's find out for sure, shall we?"

Hortense performed her examination. When she finally looked up, her smile was gentle but certain. "Congratulations, Brenda. You're going to be a mama."

A surge of excitement washed over Brenda, followed swiftly by a flood of questions. How would Seth take the news? She knew he wanted to be a father, but would he still want her to stick around once the baby was born?

"Thank you, Hortense. I—I'm not sure what to do next," Brenda confessed, her usual confidence wavering.

"Take your time, dear. This is your news to share when you're ready. And today, you have a party to host," Hortense reminded her.

"Of course, the party," Brenda said, a determined glint returning to her eye. She stood up, smoothing her skirt. "Can't have the guest of honor looking green around the gills."

"Go on now. And Brenda," Hortense added, "Seth's a good man. Whatever his preoccupations, he'll stand by you."

Brenda nodded, bolstered by Hortense's words. But she needed to know where she stood with Seth—not as his wife or the mother of his child, but as Brenda.

"Thank you, Hortense. I think I'll tell him soon. But not today." Her tone was light but resolute. "Today's about celebration."

A BASKET OF ORNAMENTS swung from Brenda's arm, and the scent of roasting meat wafted on the warm Texas breeze. She brushed a stray lock of blonde hair from her forehead and set to work, ignoring the nausea.

"All right, let's make this place shine," she muttered to herself, draping garlands along the pews with practiced ease. Her fingers worked nimbly, tying bows and arranging holly sprigs with an artist's touch.

Outside, the fire pit roasted the beef she'd talked Seth into donating for the party. Brenda tended to it, ensuring the heat cooked every side evenly. "Not bad for someone who hates to cook," she joked to no one in particular, her confidence unshaken.

The tree stood proud at the front of the church, its branches bare but for the few decorations Brenda had hung, though the bulk of them would be placed on the tree as part of the party. She stepped back, hands on hips, and surveyed the scene. "Now, isn't that pretty?" The tree waited expectantly for the baubles and trinkets that each guest would add.

As the first guests trickled in, Brenda's excitement grew. She greeted each arrival with a bright smile, her eyes twinkling with mischief.

"Evening, Mrs. Thompson," she said, handing the elder a delicate glass ornament. "Hang this up high where everyone can see."

"Thank you, dear, I will," replied Mrs. Thompson, her wrinkled face softening into a smile.

"Mr. Jenkins, sir, mind putting this star atop the tree when it's time?" Brenda asked, offering the decoration to the tall rancher.

"Would be my pleasure, Brenda," he said, hat in hand.

As more people arrived, laughter and chatter filled the air. Brenda directed them to place their gifts under the tree, making sure each present bore the right name. She was in her element—leading, organizing, bringing people together.

"John, put yours by the nativity, all right? That way we won't lose track of it," Brenda instructed John, a bashful boy with a cap too big for his head.

"Okay, Brenda," he mumbled, cheeks flushing as he did as he was told.

Every so often, Brenda's hand would subconsciously drift to her belly, a secret smile playing on her lips. Tonight was about joy, unity, and celebration.

Brenda clapped her hands lightly, drawing the attention of the bustling room. Her heart was as full as the church hall, and she couldn't help but let a genuine smile spread across her face.

"Can I have a moment?" she called out, her voice carrying over the hum of conversation. The crowd quieted, turning their eyes to her expectantly. Brenda cleared her throat, feeling a flutter in her stomach that wasn't just from nerves.

"I just want to say how much I appreciate each and every one of you for coming out tonight," Brenda began, her hands gesturing to encompass the whole gathering. "We've all worked hard to make this party happen, and look at us now—gathered here like one big family."

She paused, scanning the faces before her, recognizing the same warmth in their eyes that filled her heart. "This community, it's more than just people living side by side. It's friends, it's family, it's home. And tonight, we celebrate that spirit of togetherness. Thank you for bringing your laughter, your appetites, and your generosity."

A chorus of 'hear, hear' and applause rippled through the group, and Brenda felt a surge of pride. She gave a quick nod before stepping aside, allowing Pastor Amos to take her place at the front.

"Let us bow our heads," Pastor Amos said, his voice gentle but commanding silence with ease. Everyone complied, a quiet reverence settling over them.

"Gracious Lord," he began, "we gather here today in fellowship and gratitude. We thank You for the bounty before us, provided by the hands and hearts of this loving community. Bless the food that it may nourish us, and bless our company that it may strengthen the bonds of friendship and love among us. In Your name, we pray."

"Amen," echoed through the church, a single harmonious word binding them together.

As they raised their heads, the feast laid out on long tables beckoned. Platters of roasted meat, bowls of fresh vegetables, and baskets of homemade bread were passed around with cheer. Laughter mingled with the clinking of cutlery, and the room swelled with the joy of a shared meal and friendship.

Brenda watched the scene unfold, her heart swelling with an emotion too vast to name. She caught Seth's eye across the room, and in that glance, there was a promise—a silent understanding that no matter what lay ahead, they were in this together.

The warmth of the feast still lingered in the air as Brenda gathered a basket full of handmade ornaments, their colors bright against the woven straw. She moved among the tables, her blond hair catching the soft glow of lantern light, a smile playing on her lips.

"All right, everyone," she announced with a playful tilt of her head, "let's make that tree shine brighter than a new penny."

One by one, people ambled over to the towering evergreen that stood like a proud sentinel at the front of the church hall. Children giggled, reaching for the lowest branches, while their parents carefully selected spots higher up.

"Here you go, Pastor Amos," Brenda said, passing him a delicate angel crafted from lace and ribbon.

"Ah, thank you, Brenda. It will look divine right here," he replied, finding a place among the green needles.

"Looks like you've outdone yourself, Brenda," Seth remarked, stepping beside her with a silver star in hand.

She shrugged, a modest blush coloring her cheeks. "Just wanted to spread some cheer is all."

Seth hung the star and glanced down at her. "You always do."

With everyone pitching in, the tree was soon adorned with an eclectic mix of baubles, ribbons, and sparkling trinkets. The scent of pine mingled with the lingering aromas of supper, and the room was filled with joyous faces reflecting off shiny surfaces.

"Time for presents!" Brenda called, clapping her hands together as she made her way to the pile of gifts tucked neatly beneath the tree. Faces lit up like the lanterns overhead.

"Little Mary, this one's for you," she said, handing a neatly wrapped package to a small girl with wide eyes.

"Thank you, Mrs. Clinkinbeard!" Mary exclaimed, her voice filled with excitement as she tore into the paper to reveal a hand-carved wooden doll.

"Mr. Jenkins, catch!" Brenda tossed a smaller package to the town's blacksmith, who caught it with a surprised chuckle.

"Much obliged, Brenda," he said, unwrapping a new leather wallet.

One by one, the gifts found their recipients, each opening revealing not just a present but the thought and care the giver had put into each choice. Laughter and thanks echoed around the room, a chorus of happiness that sang of simple pleasures and heartfelt connections.

As the last gift was opened, Brenda stepped back, her heart full, watching as the community she loved basked in the warmth of the season and each other's company. She felt a contented sigh escape her, knowing this was exactly where she belonged.

Brenda watched as Susan Dailey approached, her eyes shining with a mix of gratitude and surprise. In her hands, she held the apron Brenda had made just for her.

"Brenda, this is just beautiful!" Susan exclaimed, her voice laced with sincerity as she ran her fingers over the stitching. Without another word, she wrapped Brenda in a tight embrace, the kind that spoke volumes in the absence of words.

"Couldn't have pulled off this party without your help, Susan," Brenda replied. "You're like the star atop our Christmas tree, bright and guiding."

Susan pulled back, laughing softly. "And you're the one who got the tree up in the first place! We all owe you a heap of thanks."

As the two women shared a moment of mutual admiration, the room around them buzzed with the sounds of a party in full swing. Children darted between tables, their laughter competing with the clinking of glasses and the murmur of conversations that filled the air like music.

Brenda's gaze swept over the scene, taking in the faces of friends and neighbors as they basked in the glow of fellowship. The punch bowl was never empty for long, and plates piled high with cookies seemed to replenish themselves by some Christmas miracle.

"Can't believe how well this turned out," Brenda mused aloud, a smile playing on her lips.

"Believe it. Your hard work paid off tenfold," Susan said, patting Brenda's hand reassuringly before she mingled back into the crowd.

The rest of the evening passed in a blur of contentment. Laughter rose and fell like waves, and smiles were as plentiful as the stars outside. As the night drew to a close, Brenda stood at the threshold of the church, watching as folks made their way home under the gentle guidance of moonlight.

"Wasn't this just the best Christmas party?" a young voice piped up beside her.

"Sure was, Tommy," Brenda answered, ruffling the boy's hair affectionately. "Sure was."

BRENDA LAY BESIDE SETH. Her mind buzzed with the day's triumphs, yet beneath the surface, a silent question stirred like a slumbering giant.

"Hey," she whispered, nudging Seth gently. "You awake?"

"Mhm," he murmured, his response lazy and drawn out. He turned toward her, the shadows of the room playing across his face.

"Can I ask you something?" Brenda's heart tapped a nervous rhythm against her ribs, but her tone was steady, casual even. It was how she approached all things, head-on and without pretense.

"Of course," Seth replied, propping himself up on one elbow, his attention now fully on her.

"What would you think if…well, if we couldn't have kids?" The words fell into the silence between them, heavy with the weight of her unspoken news.

Seth's brow furrowed for a moment, not in frustration but in thought. "Brenda," he began, his hand finding hers in the darkness, his grip firm and reassuring, "I married you for children, we both know that. But you not being able to have them wouldn't make me not want you in my life. Besides, it hasn't been that long. It'll happen."

"Really?" She searched his face for any sign of hesitation, but found none.

"Really." His thumb brushed softly against her skin. "Kids or no kids, it doesn't change a thing. We're in this together."

Relief washed over Brenda like a gentle wave, leaving behind it a calm that settled deep within her bones. She squeezed his hand, a silent thank you passing through the simple gesture.

"Good," she said, a soft chuckle escaping her. "That's really good to hear."

"Something on your mind?" Seth's voice carried a note of concern now, a quiet invitation for her to share more if she chose to.

"Maybe," she replied, her lips curving into a half-smile. "But not tonight. Tonight, let's just enjoy this peace."

"Sounds perfect," Seth agreed, his arm going around her.

As she drifted off to sleep, Brenda's dreams were filled with a baby, who looked just like her husband.

Chapter Thirteen

Brenda and Seth sat side by side on the porch swing, each lost in their own thoughts.

"Beautiful evening," Seth remarked.

"Sure is," Brenda replied, her gaze lingering on the horizon . She took a deep breath, feeling the weight of the moment settle in her chest. It was now or never.

She turned toward him, her green eyes locking onto his. "Seth, there's something I need to tell you," she said, her voice steady despite the flutter in her stomach.

Seth felt the shift in Brenda's posture. He peered at her, his brow furrowing slightly as he took in her earnest expression. Without a word, he reached out and enveloped her hand with his own—large, warm, calloused from years of ranch work. It was a silent vow of support, a tender gesture from a man who spoke more in actions than words.

"All right, Seth," Brenda began, drawing in another deep breath, "I've been turning things over in my mind, and I have to lay it out straight." She paused, her thumb idly stroking the back of his hand. "It's just...do you care about me at all? Or am I just convenient for you?" Her voice was steady, but her eyes searched his, hunting for truth.

Seth's grip on her hand tightened ever so slightly.

"See, I'm not sure what you really want from our marriage," Brenda's voice wavered, her usual sass softened. "I mean, a ranch needs a lady, but do you need me, Seth?"

Seth's eyes, the color of the Texas earth, never left hers. He waited, silent as the old oak tree that shadowed their modest porch.

Swallowing the lump in her throat, Brenda's next words tumbled out, more fragile than she intended. "I'm...We're going to have a baby." Her green eyes shimmered, betraying her fear. "And I'm scared, Seth. Scared you won't be in our marriage with your whole heart."

Seth's calloused hand, firm yet tender, enveloped Brenda's. "Brenda," he began, "I know I've given you reasons to doubt. I regret that more than you can imagine."

His gaze held hers, warm and sincere like the fading sunlight that bathed them both. The tension in Brenda's shoulders eased just a fraction as she listened.

"Truth is," Seth continued, "you've upended my world in ways I never saw coming." A chuckle escaped him, softening the edges of his confession. "Before you, it was all about acres and cattle. Now..." He paused, searching for the right words.

"Look at me, talking about feelings and futures." His thumb brushed over her knuckles. "You've brought something into my life I didn't even know was missing. You've made me care, Brenda, really care, about more than land and profit."

"Love and companionship," he said firmly, "are now the richest parts of my life. And they're all because of you.

"Every morning," he said, "I promise to be there. For you, for our child." He looked into her eyes. "We're in this together, Brenda. I aim to cherish every moment."

She couldn't help it—her eyes widened. In the soft glow of dusk, surprise mingled with a blossoming hope. She'd expected evasions, perhaps even excuses, but instead, Seth offered her unwavering support, a pledge to stand by her side. It was more than she'd dared to imagine.

"Really?" she whispered, her voice laced with the remnants of disbelief.

"Truly," he confirmed, and there was a smile in his voice.

The edges of her mouth twitched, then lifted, unfurling into a genuine smile.

"Thank you, Seth," Brenda said, her tone lighter, almost playful. "For a man of few words, you sure know how to make them count."

Seth's chuckle rumbled softly between them, a sound that held both relief and contentment. "I'm learning," he admitted. "And I've got the best teacher."

In the simplicity of the moment, with hearts laid bare and promises made, Brenda knew the depth of Seth's love was as vast as the Texas sky stretching endlessly above them.

"Is this real?" Brenda murmured, her words a featherlight touch against the evening air.

"Every bit of it," Seth replied.

They wrapped their arms around each other. Brenda nestled into Seth's embrace, her sharp wit and sassiness melting into the warmth of his chest. His arms tightened around her, a solid testament to his commitment.

"Whatever comes our way, we'll face it together," he said.

"Side by side," Brenda agreed.

"Look there," Seth pointed with his free hand, "first star of the evening."

"Make a wish?" Brenda asked, her voice playful yet soft, like the breeze that rustled the leaves around them.

"Already got it," he replied. "I love you, Brenda Clinkinbeard. I love you for you, and not for the baby you're carrying. I love the woman who spent weeks planning a Christmas party and days scrubbing an already clean house."

Brenda chuckled. "Oh, Seth, I love you too!" She leaned her head against Seth's shoulder.

"Never thought I'd find this," Seth finally broke the silence, his voice rich with emotion. "With you."

"Life's funny that way," Brenda replied. "Takes a turn when you least expect it."

"Guess we're proof of that," he said.

"Sure are, cowboy," Brenda teased lightly.

"Ready for whatever comes next?" Seth asked.

"Always," Brenda answered, her confidence ringing true in the quiet night.

Epilogue

Seth's heart skipped as Hortense approached, cradling the tiniest bundle he'd ever seen. His hands trembled slightly at the sight.

"Mr. Clinkinbeard," Hortense said with a soft smile, presenting the infant to him. "Meet your daughter."

He took her gently and looked down into the baby's face. Her tiny fingers curled around his, gripping with surprising strength. Seth's eyes brimmed with unspoken emotion.

"Hey there, little lady," he murmured, his voice carrying a new layer of tenderness.

Excitement propelled him through the hallways to Brenda's room. Pushing the door open, he found Brenda propped up, her blond hair framing her face in a halo despite the ordeal she'd just been through. Her green eyes met his.

"Seth, I'm sorry...it's not a boy," she whispered, a shadow crossing her features.

Seth crossed the room in three long strides, his gaze never leaving their daughter. He sat beside Brenda on the bed, careful not to jostle her. The newborn between them.

"Darling," Seth started, his voice steady and sure, "she's perfect."

Brenda's eyes searched his, seeking the truth behind his words. When she found it, her lips curved into a tired but genuine smile.

"Really?"

"Really," he said. "And besides, this just means we get to have another." A playful twinkle lit his eye, reflecting the same optimism that had seen them through so many trials.

"Another?" Brenda chuckled, the sound weak but full of life. "You do have a way with words, Mr. Clinkinbeard."

"Only the best for you, Mrs. Clinkinbeard," he replied. They both knew their journey was just beginning, but with love as their compass, they were ready to face it together.

www.ingramcontent.com/pod-product-compliance
Lightning Source LLC
Chambersburg PA
CBHW051854130726
47987CB00002B/834